AYOKA'S PROPHECY©

AYOKA'S PROPHECY©

Two young boys of different cultures meet on the Western Plains in the 1800s. They become Blood Brothers through many harrowing adventures in their fight to fulfill Ayoka's Prophecy.
"A spellbound and tension building adventure of the western plains in the 1800s, when boys had to be men and girls had to be women at an early age."

By Chastine E. Shumway

Illustrations: Sharon Baldwin

iUniverse, Inc.
New York Lincoln Shanghai

AYOKA'S PROPHECY©

iUniverse, Inc.

For information address:
iUniverse, Inc.
2021 Pine Lake Road, Suite 100
Lincoln, NE 68512
www.iuniverse.com

ISBN: 0-595-31460-0

Printed in the United States of America

This book is gratefully dedicated to GOD who has blessed me with a wonderful family who have given me
'Heaven on Earth'

To my Shumway children: Sandy, Dick, Art, Susie, Florence, Betty

To my Daughters by Marriage: Beverly and Robin Shumway

To my grandchildren: Candace, Erik, Jacob, Jennifer, Rick, Rachael, Kris, Akisha, Danielle, Breanna, Russell, Frederick, Maria, Chastine (namesake), Victoria Rose, Eddie & great-grandson Devon

In Memory of my great-uncle Julius Frederick Survivor of The Greely Expedition, 1881

And last but not least 'In Memory of 'Baby' who was my beloved granddog.

Contents

PREFACE

They say that dynamite comes in small packages. In the 1800's, four pound Julius Frederick shot out of his mother's womb as she took her last breath with his small fists clenched and his face red with fury and a thunderous cry that echoed throughout the hull of the ship.

Big German born Otto Koehler said, as he held his tiny and fragile newborn son tightly to his chest, "This little mite is going to be tough. He's destined for a life of gusto. America, here we come! We're going to the land of opportunity little feller." With tears streaming down his robust cheeks, he stooped down and kissed his lifeless wife's cold lips.

Many passengers crowded the dirty ship along with luggage, crates of salt, sugar, beef, pork, crackers, and other supplies. A cow and a few chickens were on board to provide milk and eggs for the long journey. Big Otto was determined to make it somehow to the land of plenty.

CHAPTER 1

AYOKA, THE YOUNG INDIAN BOY

Ayoka crept silently out of the teepee, hoping he wouldn't wake his snoring grandfather, Chief of the Sioux Tribe. Knowing what he had to do, he had worn his clothes to bed. He was 14 years old, and the time had come for him to prove to the Great Spirit, the Sioux tribe, and himself what kind of brave he would be. It was time for him to make his medicine. His deerskin medicine pouch hung around his neck. He had already filled it with various mosses and grasses. This medicine bag would keep him safe from the evil spirits. He would keep it with him at all times. Armed with his hickory bow plummeted with Eagle feathers his grandfather had given him, quiver, and lance, Ayoka felt brave and safe.

Wolf, his half-breed dog, licked his hand and followed Ayoka mimicking his master's quick steps to his horse, Shasta. Jumping on her Ayoka headed for Lookout Mountain to make sure all was well on the prairie before making his trip.

Feeling the wildness in Shasta's body, he gave her full rein. He was never able to break her completely, and he didn't want to. A complete abandonment would spoil their relationship. Reaching the top of Lookout Mountain, Ayoka's sharp eyes scanned the prairie. All was well. He yelled "hi-yi" as they galloped down the mountain to the plains. He felt the rhythm of Shasta's muscles moving beneath him. Wolf followed at a dead run.

DANGER AT PINNACLE

Days later they arrived at the base of Pinnacle Mountain. The majestic mountain loomed above everything else on the prairie. It was so high that its crest was shrouded in misty clouds. Ayoka dismounted Shasta, and sat down to rest before they journeyed up the mountain's rough terrain.

While resting with Wolf at his feet, his mind wandered back to his tribe. He had been warned by his grandfather not to go to Pinnacle Mountain. A few braves had gone there and never returned. Ayoka listened to the stories told by various braves of the tribe at the powwows. The more he heard, the more Ayoka secretly yearned to conquer the mystery of the mountain when he came of age. Excited by these thoughts, he jumped to his feet and leaped on Shasta urging her into a canter up the mountain.

The trail was narrow and rocky, but Shasta was sure-footed, and feeling the anticipation in her young master's body, she sped ahead. All of a sudden Shasta laid back her ears and her eyes rolled as she reared up nervously snorting loudly. Ayoka held on tightly to Shasta's neck, as they began backing down the mountain. He looked ahead. In their pathway lay a huge rattlesnake stretched to full length with its head in the wind. Panic pricked at the base of Ayoka's spine. Wolf, who had been ahead, was now belly-crawling towards the back of the snake. His hair stood on end with raised hackles, his sharp teeth bared. It happened fast. The law of nature kicked in. Wolf grabbed the back of the snake's neck, clamping his teeth onto its scaly skin shaking it furiously. He slapped it back and forth on the sharp jagged rocks until its muscles gave out. The dangerous reptile writhed no more. It was dead.

Ayoka pulled his knife from its sheath. He jerked the limp snake from Wolf, and slashed its head off. Then he flung the snake over a tree limb, marking the trail. Stroking Wolf's head affectionately, he said, "Good dog!" He jumped on Shasta's back again and headed up the trail.

Wolf charged ahead, but came whining and running back down the mountain to Ayoka, tugging on his buckskin leggings.

"What's wrong Wolf?" Ayoka asked. "Easy Shasta, easy." They slowly followed Wolf up the mountain. Wolf came to a halt staring at the remains of a human skeleton. A tomahawk was still clutched in its bony hand caked with dried blood.

The words of his grandfather rang in his brain. "The braves never returned from Pinnacle Mountain." Wolf's eyes held a pleading 'Let's go home' look.

Ayoka had never seen Wolf so spooked. In a stern voice, Ayoka said, "Wolf, go back to the camp." Pointing down the mountain path, he shoved Wolf to head him back. With a look of determination, he said, "I've come this far, and I'm not turning back." With that decision he swung to a side saddle position, leaned down from Shasta and snatched the tomahawk from the Indian's hand, then impatiently drove his heels into Shasta's sides.

Shasta's ears erect and her eyes bulging, moved into a swift trot. The trail became more twisted and rugged. Then in their pathway in full view lay a broken arrow. This was a warning sign not to go any further. Who could have done this? Ayoka looked in all directions. Wolf charged ahead, looking back at Ayoka with narrowed eyes and curled his lip into a snarl.

CHAPTER 3

THE POWERFUL VISION

It was dusk when they came to a plateau of luxuriant greenery. Ayoka swung down from Shasta. "This is a good spot to begin my fasting and sleeping, comrades."

Wolf began gulping from a stream of clear water running over a gravely bed alive with fish. Shasta's mouth was heavy with foam. She ambled over to the water satisfying her thirst, then began nibbling the grass.

Ayoka chuckled as he watched Wolf chasing a slippery trout, which had gotten away from him and was flip-flopping through the tangled grass with Wolf in hot nose pursuit.

Ayoka found a comfortable spot and began making his fasting bed. He had gathered some sweet sage and ground cedar along their journey. He burnt a root of e-say and stood in the midst of the smoke smearing his body with sage. He sat down in cross-leg Indian style facing the direction of the all-powerful sun "Wakonda". Rocking back and forth, he chanted to the Great Spirit. His cry echoed through the night and into the early morning. He drifted into a trance-like sleep. While Ayoka was in this period of unknown danger and abstinence, the Great Spirit was at work. He began to dream.

In the dream Ayoka saw himself with another boy about his age hunting buffalo. Out of nowhere a huge white buffalo bull appeared. He charged towards both boys, his oversized shaggy head bent down low. In his dream a river of swirling blood appeared. A low deep voice spoke, "It is not a good day to die, Ayoka. Go my Mentor and wear me well. I am your Protector."

The vision's power surged through his body. Ayoka knew the mighty sacred white buffalo would be his mysterious protector throughout his life. He was the wisest and most powerful of all creatures. He was a symbol of leadership, long life, and plenty.

J. Baldwin

CHAPTER 4

KIDNAPPED BY GOLDIE

Ayoka's senses were reeling as he slowly awakened from his dream. He felt like he was being carried through the air. It felt as if claws were embedded into his shoulders. He heard Wolf's howling far away. He must open his eyes. It was time to go back to his Grandfather's lodge and tell him of his vision. His body was churning. He was dizzy. He opened his eyes. He was airborne and was whizzing through space at the speed of an antelope, towards the heavens, towards the peak of Pinnacle Mountain. He twisted and wiggled. He must get loose now! He could not loosen the grip. Kerplunk! Ouch! It felt as if swords and knives were piercing his back and behind.

A monstrous gold-feathered bird stood over him. It was the sacred Golden War Eagle, the god that banged on the noisy drums with flashes of light zigzagging across the heavens. She had carried him to her nest, a nest made out of sharp sticks, bones, and feathers.

The Golden War Eagle was known among the Indians to be a courageous bird. He thought to himself, am I going to be a sacrifice for this sacred bird? He decided he would just play dead right now.

"Ouch!" He jumped! That idiot bird yanked one of his black hairs from his head. Ayoka squinted one eye barely open to see what Goldie was doing. She was just as curious as he was. With her big curved beak and her beady eyes she was examining him from head to toe with a strand of hair hanging from her beak. He'd get even with her later. I'll scalp her, he thought, and take her feathers as another coup. She plummeted out of her nest, swooping downwards, with a loud scream of victory over her trophy.

Ayoka looked over the edge of the nest. He could see nothing but thick masses of white clouds with a deep narrow opening, where Goldie had streaked through. Ayoka began chanting and crying to the Great Spirit to save him. His wailing stretched out beyond the mountains, through the canyons and the plains.

Wolf, hearing his master's cry raised his head towards the mountain peak uttering long mournful howls.

Shasta who had been napping pricked her ears up at the sound of her master's voice and Wolf's howling. She tossed her long jet-black mane. Her eyes were fiery red. She pumped her nostrils and snorted. She sensed unknown danger in the air. Rearing up on her hind legs, she neighed mightily. Then she bolted down the mountain at a furious lope for help!

CHAPTER 5

FREDERICK, THE GERMAN BOY

The Western plains was Otto's dream fulfilled. It gave the promise of a good life he had dreamed of for him and his son. The United States Government encouraged immigrants and others to come West by offering free land to them. After the ship docked in Independence, Missouri, called the 'jumping off place', it took months to cross the Oregon Trail to the Far West by covered wagon. Otto acquired 160 acres of land under The Homestead Act, and all he had to pay for it was a sum of ten dollars registration fee and pledge to live on it for 5 years. Then the land would be his. He knew he had made the right decision on bringing his son to America!

The choice tract of wilderness land Otto chose was near a flowing river and a clear spring. Part of the property was covered with a forest of towering cottonwood trees where all kinds of wild life were abundant. The terrain was covered with bench grass, and patches of sagebrush.

When Big Otto settled on the plains, he had two horses, two oxen and a cow, Gretchen. He brought his rifle for providing food and protection. He also brought sharp knives and an ax for constructing a cabin. He had a hoe for gardening and an iron cooking pot to cook vegetables in. Frederick was almost six months old when they arrived at their land. The covered wagon continued to serve as their home until spring came.

Spring finally arrived. The trees on their property were budding, and the grass was carpeted with wild flowers in hues of yellows, blues and lavender. The "raising" of a cabin brought out all of the settlement. Children scampered around the adults full of bustling activity. One of the old men played a mouth organ. The younguns danced and sang. Building a cabin was a social event out on the lonely prairie.

C H A P T E R 6

JAKE, THE MOUNTAIN MAN

When the log 'raisin' began, Jake, a mountain man came traipsing down the mountain path with his shoulders piled high with all kinds of furs. The first thing you noticed about him was a powder-flask and bullet pouch made from buffalo horns slung around his neck. He also had a gun in his belt. On his head he was wearing a beaver cap. Although he had a scraggly beard and long yellow hair and a red twitching mustache, there was a special dignity about him in spite of all his ruggedness. His piercing gray eyes beneath his bushy eyebrows seemed to look right through you. His voice was deep and gruff. Jake was a backwoodsman who lived in a cave up the mountain. He was a rough and tough character but straightforward. He had done a lot of hard living. You could tell that by his lined face. But what startled everyone was he had a missing ear. Claimed he lost it in a b'ar fight. He was an ugly but likeable character.

"Hello neighbor," he said reaching out his hand and shaking Otto's hand vigorously. He pointed to young lass who was trying to console Frederick with a bottle of milk. She wasn't having any luck. "Looks like you need some help in putting up a cabin with that bawlin' youngun over thar." He strode over to them and took his beaver skinned hat off and tickled Frederick's chin with it. Frederick stuck his lower lip out into a pout, but then burst in to a little laugh. He grabbed the beaver tail, and held it tightly. He kept it the rest of the day. The only way Big Jake got it back was when the little lad went to sleep. Otto was glad to see a big strapping fellow like him come along.

"You bettcha. Need all the help I can get, especially a muscle-bound feller like you. Putting his hand on one of his powerful bulging arm biceps, he yelled, "Jumpin Jerusalem!"

Jake laughed. And his laugh was as big as he was. The other men who had been helping Otto came over and were impressed with this mountain man's contour of his tattooed strong muscular arms too. Nothing would do but before they continued building the cabin, they each had to arm-wrestle him. He took them down one by one.

Finally one of the women came over to where they were congregating, saying, "There will be no vittles for you lazy men if you don't get on with your work."

Looking over at the fire going with a big black pot bubbling over with stew, Jake stood up and said, "Ma'am, I smelt that stew cookin' way up on that thar mountain yonder. He pointed at the tree-covered mountain behind the log house they were building. "For those good vittles I'll be glad to help you!" Then all the men ran over to the stew filling their bowls.

It wasn't long until they stood a little ways back from the cabin looking at the progress they had made. It took a lot of sweat and hard work, but it was finally finished. Otto felt relieved that he and Frederick would soon have a good roof over their heads. It took them three days to build a one-room cabin with a loft, which was reached by a ladder, and an impressive fireplace built with fieldstones and mud stretched across one end of the single room cabin. It served for both heating and cooking. The women initiated the fireplace and served meals for the workers and a festive pull-together atmosphere prevailed.

When sundown came, Jake stuck a pine tree in the ground. One of the bearded backwoodsmen had brought a fiddle and they doe si doed and filled their bellies with food for hours into the night. The mountains and valleys echoed with the spirited music. At dawn the workers with their families climbed in their wagons and headed home.

Without any warning Jake showed up the next morning with an ax in hand, and while Otto fed the animals he built a lean-to. "The animals need protection from the changes in the weather of the plains," he said. "Later on I'll help you build a barn." And he did.

CHAPTER 7

A NEW FRIENDSHIP

Jake and Otto became fast friends. He was a trapper who knew the trails and hidden passes of the Great plains. They hunted together for deer, turkey, rabbits, and bear. Jake taught Otto how to skin the game they killed. Then they carefully salted and stretched the hides.

As Frederick grew older he went berry picking in the summer with Jake. He told Frederick, "This is where the bears like to hang out." Jake was teaching Frederick to be cautious. Jake always carried a gun. Frederick took his toy gun with them.

Otto trusted him completely. Many a night, they would eat supper together, sharing their experiences. In the spring Jake left with pelts he had trapped during the winter. He came back in the fall with his pockets jingling and various items he had traded for.

A warm relationship developed between Frederick and Unk Jake. Jake had lost his wife and little son in an Indian raid and was quite taken by little Frederick. He warned Otto to watch his little one carefully in this wild unpredictable country. He confided in Otto one evening that while he was on a trading trip, some Indians who had been drinking firewater killed his wife and small son.

If he heard any strange birdlike sounds, he immediately sheltered Frederick, as if he were a mother hen. He had keen eyesight and no matter where they went he took his gun. His eyes never rested.

When Frederick was small, Jake and Otto took him fishing with them at the river that bordered their land. One day while Frederick was playing in the river sands while they fished, Jake noticed him playing with a piece of shinny metal. He said, "By gosh, Otto I think your son has found gold." He stuck it between his teeth chomping down on it. When he went to town, he found out that it was real gold. Rushing back to Otto's cabin, he said, "Sure 'nuff' friend, thar's real gold and you've got a river full of it."

With this find, Otto was able to buy some sheep to raise for food and clothing. He shared the find with Jake.

CHAPTER 8

LONESOME NIGHTS

Living on the plains during the day doing all the chores and taking care of Frederick kept both of the men busy, but the silence of the night made the plains lonely. That was thinkin' time and loneliness of the plains would set in.

Jake said one night, "Otto we need a woman, a good woman and a mother for little Frederick."

Looking at the picture of his wife on the fireplace, Otto said wistfully, "Jake, a good woman is hard to find."

As Jake and Otto's friendship deepened, it helped both of them become less lonely. After Frederick went to bed, these two grown men would sit at the big oak table and arm wrestle by the flickering light of the fire, or play a game of Checkers. They drank strong coffee and 'chewed the fat until late at night.

News of Jake, a man who lived in a cave in the mountains with biceps as big as pumpkins traveled through the plains like wild fire. Word of his arm-wrestling skill spread throughout the territory. Men came from all over the territory to challenge this man in arm-wrestling. Jake always won.

CHAPTER 9

THE SURPRISE TRADE

As time went on, Jake introduced Otto to the friendly Sioux Indians who lived in the Black Hills. Otto soon became good friends with Chief Big Horn. He would come with some of his tribe; their horses pulling travois' loaded with items to trade.

One day, the chief brought a pretty young olive skinned Indian woman with them. Her long hair was jet black and her blue eyes were startling. Otto noticed that she was very short, about 5 feet tall. The chief made a sign that he was giving her to Otto as a gift. He said, "Ha cheena tum per" (She is young). Her name is Wee One. He pointed to her stature and sparkling eyes. He made signs with his hands that she could help Otto with his chores and in raising the chin cha (child).

Otto did not refuse taking the girl. It would be an insult to the Chief. He gave some sheep's wool in return to the Chief for his tribe. Using his hands, Otto tried to explain how Indian women could make clothing out of the wool. He gave them some young sheep, explaining that they could use them for food also. This made the Chief very happy, but he and his braves laughed at Otto's attempt at sign language.

After Wee had lived with them for awhile, much to Otto's surprise, she began to speak English. She explained to Otto that her Indian mother and French father, a trader, had died of the flu. Chief Big Horn was her Grandfather. He was very proud of her, because she could speak English as well as the Sioux language. Chief Big Horn would take her into the lodge meetings when he met with traders and government officials. She was used as an interpreter and had been an important part of negotiations.

Otto patted her cheek saying, "So that's where those blue eyes came from, your French father."

Wee One turned out to be an excellent friend and helper to Otto and Frederick.

There was one problem though. The one room log cabin was too small to include three people. Otto had to sleep up in the loft with Frederick, and Wee's bed was in the combined living room and kitchen. So one morning early he and Jake shouldered their axes and went to the woods to chop enough trees to add two more rooms. Wee and Frederick were very excited to see their small cabin turn into a log house. Now Wee had her own room and Otto had his. They moved the beds out of the one room kitchen-combined living room. Wee adapted very well to the paleface way of living and Otto and Frederick learned many things from her Indian and French heritage.

Every spring they all worked together planting a garden. As Otto turned over the ground with the oxen, Wee and Frederick followed behind, planting the seeds in the furrows. They planted sister vegetables as Wee called them, the corn, beans and squash. They also grew sunflowers for food. The birds liked these seeds. Otto and Wee laughed when the gangly sunflowers got so tall, much taller than Frederick did. He was afraid of them and wouldn't go near them. Wee said, "I wish the birds felt like Frederick does."

One day Frederick said, "I am almost big enough to help you Pa."

"If you eat your breakfast of boiled oats, Wee fixes you every morning son, you will be able to help soon. Oats is what make our animals so powerfully strong, you know," his father explained.

"Then I will eat lots of oats," Frederick said with determination. Wee glanced at Big Otto and smiled. They both knew Frederick was a determined boy who had a mind of his own at this early age. He learned quickly.

One day Wee said, "Vegetables are important in a garden, but it would be so nice to see some flowers from the south window.

Otto smiled, "Yes, we must have some flowers for a woman's touch."

Wee blushed when he teased her.

Turning to Frederick, he said, "Son you are big enough now to help Wee with her flower planting."

Wee also added a special magical garden of various herbs. Her Indian heritage had taught her that certain herbs, roots, barks, and berries were used for medicinal brews and extracts. It was evidently the belief that the stronger they tasted and smelled the more effective they would be. She and Frederick would go out into the forest and strip slippery Elm trees of their bark and made a heavy salve. This was good for bullet wounds and infected sores. When Frederick had the measles with a high fever, Wee steeped some of her herbs and gave him a teaspoon now and then. It broke the fever. When anyone felt sick, she got her home remedies out which were mixed with her Indian background of superstition. She would use her medicinal concoction, curing any one who was under the weather.

Through the years, before Wee put Frederick to bed, she told him stories about her brother, Ayoka, who was a year younger than Frederick. She said that one day she would take him to the Indian Village and introduce them to each other, but she never did. She taught Frederick and Big Otto the Sioux language. Theirs was a happy lifestyle.

Sometimes she would disappear, and Frederick and Otto missed her at these times very much. They knew she was visiting her grandfather and friends in the Black Hills. She usually made her trips at the end of the summer.

CHAPTER 10

A GOOD RELATIONSHIP

Several years passed, and now Frederick was 15 years old and was finally able to help his Pa with the more manly chores about the farm. He had grown into a handsome lad. He had a dark complexion, a shock of black unruly hair and penetrating dark brown eyes.

Wee tanned the hide from a deer Frederick had killed, and made him leggings and moccasins. She made shirts that hung freely over his hips. He was very proud of an ornate belt Wee had made him from beads that had belonged to his Mother. Frederick looked more Indian than Wee did.

He could handle a long smoothbore rifle as well as any grown man. Loading and sighting and firing his gun became a normal instinctive action. Frederick was known as being an excellent shot. Unk Jake taught him how to set traps and how to be very careful that he didn't get any of his body parts in their sharp teeth. Frederick now accompanied Jake to the town trading post in the spring and earned money by selling his furs too.

CHAPTER 11

GYPSY A ONE MAN'S HORSE

One of Frederick's favorite past times was riding his spirited Appaloosa horse, Gypsy. She was a sleek black mare with a white spotted blanket over her loin and hips. She had a white apron marked face and white stockings. He could ride bareback like an Indian as well as with a saddle with her.

Most Appaloosa horses were known for their sweet dispositions, but Gypsy was her own horse. She could be very good but if the situation demanded it she could be stubborn as a mule. Frederick and Gypsy got along fine, because they were of the same material. When there was spare time, Wee, Otto, and Frederick would race each other on the wide-open plains.

Big Otto proudly said that Wee was a perfect frontierswoman. He also said, "Some Indian Brave will be very lucky to get her for his woman."

Wee remained silent and looked downcast when he said this. Big Otto interpreted this as her being shy.

CHAPTER 12

THE WHITE BUFFALO BULL

One chilly night, when Frederick and his father were tending the chores, Wee sounded the angle iron from the cabin door. Supper was ready. It wasn't long until they were washing up in the basin. Wee noticed Frederick's muscular arms and how his shoulders rippled as he dried himself with the towel. He was his own man now at the age of fifteen. How fast time had passed. There was pride in her eyes. He had grown into a good strong man like his father. He was lean and muscular and sure-handed with tools and guns. They sat down at the table of deer meat, beans, and cornbread. Otto gave thanks to the Great Father. Frederick was unusually quiet. All of a sudden he jumped up and left the table pacing the floor.

Wee looked upset. "Is the food not good Frederick?"

Otto said, "Sit down my son, and eat your food. You've put in a good day's work, and you need some hot food in that belly of yours."

"There's nothing wrong with the meal, but I have the jitters tonight. I can't put my finger on it, but something out there on the prairie isn't right. It's calling to me." He rubbed his chin, which he always did when troubled.

Somewhat baffled at his grave tone, Otto got up from the supper table. "Me too son. I feel the same uneasy way. When the wind blew just right, I heard a weird chanting and howling. It seemed to be coming from Pinnacle Mountain. "That mountain has a weird effect on everything throughout the plains."

Wee shuddered and spoke in a hushed voice. "I've heard it for days now. There's danger in the wind."

"I'm going outside and look around." Grabbing his gun from the wall, Frederick walked towards the door unlatching it. Otto followed Frederick with his gun too. "Look," Frederick said excitedly and pointed to a huge form standing in the light of a full moon. "A white buffalo! I've never seen one before."

Wee ran to where Frederick stood. She grabbed his arm, tugging and pulling him back towards the cabin door. Fred stubbornly refused to move.

The large white bull stood watching them and pawing the ground with steam shooting from his nostrils. He roared and snorted. The earth trembled.

"It's an omen!" Wee whispered in a frightened voice.

In a calm authoritative voice, Otto walked over and said, "Git to the house. I will kill him." He slowly raised his gun to his shoulder.

Wee grabbed his arm, saying, "No, Otto, do not kill him. He is trying to warn us, trying to tell us something. To see a grand white bull such as this is very special. Please let him be."

Otto lowered his gun. They all walked quickly to the house, all but Frederick who hesitated before deciding to turn and follow them. The big bull stood his ground, as if he had a purpose. Frederick crawled into his bed. He was uneasy and found it hard to sleep.. He tossed and turned all night, sometimes getting up and glancing out the window. The white buffalo stayed a long time.

CHAPTER 13

JOURNEY WITH GAMBLER'S GHOST

Morning came early for all of them, so early that it was still dark. Wee was already working in the kitchen. Otto had gotten up earlier and started a fire. He had also checked to see if the white buffalo was there. It was gone.

When Frederick came into the kitchen, ham and eggs were already sizzling on the stove. As soon as they had eaten, Frederick said, "Pa, I couldn't sleep most of the night. I aim to go to Pinnacle Mountain."

Wee spoke in a low voice. "That mountain is haunted. Our braves who went there never returned. Frederick that mountain is sacred!"

Frederick said, "Something just isn't right. I have to go Wee."

Wee walked over to the stove, pouring a cup of Indian coffee and handed it to him. She knew that they could not change Frederick's mind. The love of adventure was in his blood and bones.

"Drink this coffee before you go. You will freeze if you do not warm up good first."

"Thank you Wee. "It is a very cold morning, and I shall need all the warmth I can start out with. Last night when I was sure you were all asleep, and the bull left, I prepared Gypsy for our trip. I also decided to take Chop Stix with us. I will need him to carry extra supplies."

Chop Stix was a skinny mule who showed up at their place one morning. Now Chop Stix was not just another mule. He was an albino white mule. He had blood red stripes of a whip across his rump. Frederick doctored him up, and they became close friends, as close as an obstinate mule and boy can be. Gypsy was jealous of the little mule but put up with him as long as he stayed out of her way. Big Jake got a big kick out of Chop Stix, and he called him a gambler's ghost. He told Frederick that Chop Stix would be his lucky charm.

Wee walked over to a large cedar chest and took out quilts she had made. "You will need these for warmth." She had already packed a large basket for him filled with lots of cornbread, hardtack, pemmican and some dried fruit. She also packed him a huge canteen of Indian coffee. In his personal bundle she tucked a small jar of the Elm Magic Salve.

Frederick walked over to Wee. Putting his arm around her, he stooped down and brushed his lips against her hair. "Your hair has the sweet scent of the earth after a fresh rain. I love you like a sister, little one. Don't worry about me. I'll be all right."

"I'm against it son, but I won't stand in your way." Frederick went over to his father giving him a vigorous hug and a pat on the back. Quickly he headed out the door. He mounted Gypsy with his gun slung over his thighs in a cover of buckskin. He adjusted his red bandana around his nose. It was windy and it would keep the dust out of his face. Besides carrying his gun, he had several knives and an ax with him. Chop Six followed noisily with the blanket roll, cooking utensils and other gear.

Wee wiped a tear from her eye. Otto had never seen Wee show any emotion. Surprised, he walked over to where she stood and put his arm around her. They stood for a long time listening to the thundering of Gypsy and Chop Stix's hooves. They watched them cross the stream, waving a last good-by before they vanished into the heavy timber.

CHAPTER 14

ARRIVAL AT PINNACLE MOUNTAIN

Frederick goaded Gypsy on. Gypsy was a one-man horse who was hotheaded and would go into a bucking frenzy if anyone but Frederick tried to ride her. She and Frederick had won trophies in bull riding, calf roping, steer wrestling and lassoing. She could pivot, spin, or make other sudden changes of speed quickly. With the slightest pressure of the reins or the movement of Frederick's legs, Gypsy got the message. They became one.

He slapped Gypsy on her rear and hollered "Giddap! Faster!" The mare stretched her neck and raced at full gallop over the plains. Fred's hat flew off with the string holding it around his neck. The wind whistled past his ears whipping through his thick black hair. They were now part of the freedom of the prairie, a land that stretched as far as the eye could see. Chop Stix barely kept the pace with his clattering pans.

Days later, the magnificent Pinnacle Mountain rose in the distance. When they arrived at the mountain, the sun was dropping close to the mountains. Fred heard wolves baying in the distance.

He patted Gypsy's neck, saying, "We'll go up a piece until we find a stream and quench our thirst." He reined Gypsy up the rocky terrain. It wasn't long until they came to a small stream. Frederick dismounted Gypsy. He picketed Chop Stix by a nearby tree. He built a fire by rubbing flint stones together. The blaze of the fire lit up the area.

Leading Gypsy to the water, he jumped back. The stream was filled with blood. Gypsy reared up. Her eyes laid back and her nostrils puffed in and out. She snorted. "Easy, Gypsy, Easy!" In the distance wolves were howling and fighting viciously. Spasmodic barks, snorts, and yelps announced the battle was still on. Wherever the blood was coming from, the wolf culprits had the spoils. Frederick took his canteen out, poured some water in his hat, giving Gypsy and Chop Stix a drink. He took his gun and fired once into the air. A deafening silence prevailed.

In disregard for his own safety he walked up the path with his gun cocked. Something slimy slapped his face. He fired his gun into the air again to warn any living creature he meant business. He turned and walked back to sit by the fire half-dozing until dawn. The air was silent except for the sound of the wind and the snoring of the horses.

CHAPTER 15

DEATH ABOUNDS

The morning at sun-up, Frederick checked the bloody stream. It had cleared up to a light pink. That meant a gushing spring was nearby. Then the blood began to pound in his head. His chest felt tight. He could hardly breathe at what he saw. A beautiful sorrel mare lay dead alongside the stream. Shivers sped up and down his spine. So that's what the wolves were fighting over! He could tell the mare had put up a good fight. One gray wolf lay dead, and the way the dirt looked, there had been a tough scuffle. The mare didn't have a chance with those sneaky, greedy animals, especially at night. The vultures were gawking and their heavy stooped bodies were sitting above his head on the barren tree limbs waiting impatiently to swoop down and devour the leftovers.

Frederick looked around for a rider. A huge dangling snake hung from a branch. Its head had been slashed off. So that is what brushed against his face last night. He found a long lariat and someone's saddlebag on the ground. Several questions were popping through Frederick's mind. Who killed the snake? Where was the rider of the beautiful sorrel? He quickly went back and put the hot coals out.

Gypsy and Chop Stix were anxious to continue their journey. Gypsy was looking at Chop Stix with a look that said, "Why did we have to bring you? You're only in the way."

Frederick slung the looped rope and mysterious saddlebag on Chop Stix' back. The mule looked at Gypsy as if to say, "See, I am needed too." Gypsy turned her head giving Chop Stix the cold shoulder. Frederick mounted Gypsy, and they headed to fresh water and refilled the canteens. The horses gleefully splashed and drank the water until they quenched their thirst. Chop Stix felt frisky now, but kept his distance from Gypsy. She was almost friendly to him as they had a little horseplay earlier, but Gypsy had a habit of nipping him, if he ventured too close. She only wanted him when she was in the mood to play. That was a mare for you, he thought. He knew Gypsy thought he would spook easily. But he would show her sometime just what a gutsy little mule could do.

Refreshed they continued their journey. Suddenly Gypsy came to an abrupt halt moving her head back and forth, then stabilizing it to the right. Frederick looked down at the ground. There lay the bones of a dead corpse with a broken arrow beside him. Then from a distance they heard a weak voice chanting the death song. Frederick urged Gypsy into a faster trot.

CHAPTER 16

KICKING BUTT WINS OVER CULPRIT

Late in the afternoon they came to a glen with green grass and trees. The horses were sweaty and tired, and so was Frederick. Frederick swung his leg over to dismount. A yell pierced the air. It was Frederick's. A fierce pain shot up his leg. He plunged forward and hit the ground. A wolf jumped in front of him snarling. He was ready to attack him again. Gypsy reared on her hind legs. Then a crazy "E-e-e-e-onk! E-e-e-e-onk!" Chop Stix raced to the rescue and braying loudly charged between the wolf and Frederick. The pots and pans clashed noisily. He turned his butt around and with his back hoofs raised high in the air he began furiously kicking the white wolf. The wolf went spinning like a top through the air. The air was filled with a fog of dust from all the commotion.

The wolf was so confused with the entire racket of pots and pans and a big butt with kicking feet, that when he landed on his head, he was stunned. Frederick could not help but remember that Unk Jake had said that Chop Stix would be his lucky charm.

Frederick, his back on the ground, quickly reached for his lariat. Lifting his pain racked body up; he carefully swung the coiled rope with all of the strength he could muster. It lassoed the wolf's head.

Frederick called Gypsy to him and commanded, "Kneel!" Then he wrapped the rope around the saddle horn. Gypsy knew what to do. She stood at a distance allowing no slack in the rope. The wolf tugged and struggled with all his might like a cantankerous bull. He put all of his strength in a last tug for freedom, but the rope had slid down around his neck, the pressure choking him. He made a low throaty gurgling growl. Then he swooned. Gypsy proudly stood still waiting for Frederick to remove the rope. Frederick grabbed his gun. He was going to shoot the varmint.

CHAPTER 17

❀

THE SURPRISE
ACQUAINTANCE

Frederick aimed the gun and cocked it. A feeble cry broke through the deafening silence of the mountain. "Here Wolf, here Wolf, get help." A weak voice cried the death chant.

Wee had taught Frederick the Sioux language, and he understood the Indian. He laid the gun down and cupped his hand over his mouth and called in Sioux tongue. "I am here to do everything within my power to save you. But first I must doctor my leg. Your wolf dog thought it was a meaty bone!" There was a silence. He called, "Where are you?"

"Harte, Har, Har. His name is Wolf, and I am Ayoka. You're not an Indian brave, if you let a dog bite stop you. Harte, Har, Har. The golden eagle has me as a prisoner in her nest at the peak of this mountain."

Frederick was in shock. The name, Ayoka. That is Wee's brother's name. "Well at least I'm not a prisoner of an eagle," he yelled. "Harte, Har, Har." He limped over to where Wolf was and wrapped the rope around a nearby tree several times. He put some fresh meat and water near him. Then he threw water on Wolf's face from a distance. Wolf came to. Narrowing his eyes, he looked suspiciously at Frederick, Gypsy, and Chop Stix, and lunged again and again towards them but the rope flipped him backwards.

Chop Stix brayed, as if he were laughing. Wolf growled, until he was hoarse. Being hungry and completely tired out, he finally consumed the food with frightening voracity.

Frederick went to the stream and washed the blood off his leg. Then tied apiece of cloth around a birch limb (making a tourniquet), turning it and releasing it at intervals to stop the bleeding. He reached into his personal bundle and pulled out the Elm Magic Salve Wee had thoughtfully packed and rubbed some on the bite. The horses cropped on the grass. Chop Stix rolled over on his back, scratching it on the brush. Gypsy walked over to Chop Stix and nuzzled him. She looked at him with a new respect in her big eyes. She hadn't realized what a brave little mule he was. Then she stood motionless, napping.

Chop Stix let out a big guffaw, Heehaw! He vowed right then and there that someday he would cut her down to his size. Yep he had plans for them in the near future!

CHAPTER 18

ALL IS NOT LOST

In the eagle's nest, Goldie was treating Ayoka like an eaglet, bringing him wild animals to eat and some fish. When Goldie left in the mornings, Ayoka would throw most of the smelly food out of the nest. He was getting weaker by the minute. But now there was hope. Someone was going to help him. But who was this person who was brave enough or stupid enough to come on Pinnacle Mountain?

Frederick felt much better after he rested. His leg was still sore, but he could walk a little better. He looked over at Wolf, and said, "Hello Wolf." Wolf looked surprised, when he heard his name. "Your master, Ayoka thought it was funny when I told him you had bitten me." Wolf's ears perked up at the name of Ayoka. He whined and wagged his tail.

Frederick limped over to him slowly. Reaching his hand into his pockets, he took some cornbread crumbs out. Wolf licked the crumbs from Frederick's palm. "Well, I guess this means we are going to be friends." Frederick patted Wolf's head. "Let's see." He untied the rope around Wolf's neck. Then he turned his back and went over to the stream and put his leg in the water. The sun had warmed the water, and it felt very good. Wolf walked over cautiously and lay down beside Frederick laying his head in his lap.

Frederick rubbed his chin. He had to save Ayoka, and it had to be quick. By nightfall he had his plans made for the rescue.

CHAPTER 19

THE PLAN

At daybreak, the comrades continued their perilous journey up the rough terrain of Pinnacle. Frederick planned to go as far as he could by horseback. Wolf led the way. The incline of the mountain was hazardous. The higher they went, the colder it got. Soon they came to a plateau where they stopped to camp. Gypsy and Chop Stix' hooves were bleeding, and they couldn't continue the journey. Frederick drove Gypsy and Chop Stix up to the mouth of a gulch where the grass was lush and thick. When he left them they were grazing placidly.

Going back to their camp, Frederick shaded his eyes from the sun, and looking upward saw a protruding jagged cliff. This would be perfect for his plans, but he would have to go it alone. Maybe he would make it, but maybe he wouldn't. He had to make it for Ayoka's sake! With hatchet in hand, ropes, knives, hard bread, and canteen of coffee in his backpack, he was ready. Turning to Wolf he said in a commanding voice. "Stay!" He began climbing the rocky mountain. He used his sharp ax, burying its head into the rocks as he climbed higher and higher towards the ledge. Although it was cool, his thick head of hair was drenched with sweat. He stuck his tongue out catching the salty moisture as it rolled down his face. The way became more rugged and difficult. Being dog-tired and tuckered out, he finally used every bit of energy and strength he had left to pull his aching body onto the protruding ledge. He lay laboriously breathing, then fell into a deep swoon.

CHAPTER 20

THE RESCUE

Frederick came to with something rough and cool swishing his face. It was wolf, licking him. "Wolf, I'm sure glad you didn't obey orders. I need your help! But, hey! There has to be another way to get to this point and you know the way. You sly old dog!" He got up and started exploring the ledge. He discovered a cave. "Just what we need," he said. Then looking upward he cupped his mouth and called to Ayoka. "When the eagle leaves her nest, whistle."

It wasn't long until a shrill whistle rode the sound waves.

"Wolf, we have to work fast." Just then a hare slumped through the brush. He said, "Get it Wolf! Wolf grabbed it by the nape of its neck, taking it to Frederick. He patted Wolf's head. "Good dog!" Then Frederick tied the kicking hare to one end of a rope. Just then, Goldie plunged through the clouds. She began circling. Her keen eyes spotted Wolf. She nose-dived towards him.

Frederick twirled the rope swinging it upward with the rabbit on the end of it and swung it over Goldie's head. Goldie diverted her attention to the wiggling rabbit. She made an upward dip and seized it with her huge sharp claws. She carried the hare and dangling rope up to her nest. Her scream of victory echoed loudly.

Frederick and Wolf jumped up and down together. "It worked Wolf, it worked! Now it's up to Ayoka!" The two comrades headed quickly to the mouth of the cave.

When Goldie landed back into the nest with her catch, Ayoka stroked her wings. The rope, which was attached to the rabbit, was very long. Ayoka figured out why. That night when Goldie was roosting, he tied the rope around her thighs and put the other end of the rope around his waist. Ayoka was ready for the ride of his life.

Early the next morning at daybreak, Goldie left for the hunt. She knew exactly what she was after. She tumbled out of her nest, screeching, half-flying, half falling through the air. She could not figure out what seemed to be an added weight to her flight. Ayoka held on for dear life swinging and tumbling through the clouds. Then Goldie saw her target. She headed for Wolf. Frederick and Wolf were ready for her. Ayoka came dangling on the end of the rope, and as he swung towards Frederick, he grabbed him and quickly cut the rope from his waist. "Run Ayoka! Follow Wolf to the cave!" Ayoka tore up the path following Wolf. Goldie, squawking loudly at her unexplainable disastrous flight, slammed into the ledge. While she was dazed, Frederick quickly tied her big clawed feet together.

CHAPTER 21

BLOOD BROTHERS

Frederick walked to the cave where Ayoka was hungrily gobbling the hard dried biscuits, shoving them into his mouth with both hands. Frederick handed him some hot coffee. He asked him, "Are you Wee's brother?" As they talked, their voices echoed weirdly throughout the musty cave.

Ayoka with chipmunk filled cheeks just grunted. "Ugh!" He was too hungry to answer. As he swallowed the food, he looked at Frederick with a puzzled look. Frederick laughed saying, "That eagle food must have been rotten."

Ayoka nodded his head up and down, saying "Aho." (Means Amen Brother). Frederick sat down in cross-legged Indian style on the floor of the cave beside Ayoka and began talking. Ayoka was surprised to hear his sister was part of Frederick's family. When he was able to talk, he said, "Frederick, I owe you my life. First you are part of my sister, and now you have saved me from death. We will become blood brothers." He looked at Frederick in a solemn manner. "Do you want to be my blood brother?"

Frederick stared at him looking puzzled. Speaking hesitantly he said, "I feel that we are brothers already, especially since Wee is your sister."

"No Frederick, we are not brothers yet. We must perform a ceremony mixing our blood together. Then we shall be blood brothers." He continued in a tense, hoarse whisper. "Do you mind an Indian being your brother?"

In a dead serious voice, Frederick said, "Ayoka, I want to become your brother." Frederick felt so warm and happy inside. He had always wanted a brother, and here was an Indian youth that wanted to be his brother.

Ayoka, his hawk like Indian expressionless face took a knife from his pocket. The blade of the knife looked exceedingly sharp. Frederick's heart began to thump. Should he trust this new brother to be?

Ayoka reached over and took hold of Frederick's wrist. He looked at Frederick and said in a low voice, "Trust me brother to be." Then with the tip of the blade, without wincing he pierced his own wrist first. "Now hold out your arm."

Without fear and complete trust, Frederick held his arm out. Ayoka pricked it. As the blood oozed out, they placed their wrist together intermingling their blood. Then clasping their hands together and raising their fist into a viselike clench they yelled, "Blood brothers, forever!" Ayoka said, "Now we are of one blanket."

They spent hours talking to each other about their hazardous adventure. Ayoka told Frederick how he had left his grandfather's lodge and went into a trance and had a vision that a white buffalo was to be his protector. Then before he came out of the trance, Goldie, the war eagle snatched him up and carried him to her nest.

Shaking his head, Frederick said, "It's strange you dreamed about a white buffalo. The night before I left to see what was going on at this mountain, a huge white bull was near our home, just standing in the moonlight. The morning I left to come to the mountain, he was gone." He grew silent. "Ayoka, this is weird. It's as if this was meant to be, planned ahead of time by an unforeseen force." He shivered. Then he mentioned the sorrel mare to Ayoka, which had been killed and consumed by the wolves.

Ayoka jumped up very upset. His eyes widened in shock. "No!" He began using his hands as he spoke in an animated way. "That horse was mine. Shasta was my best friend." His voice became depressed as he continued. "For many moons I watched a band of wild horses from a distance. This strawberry sorrel was the fastest runner of the bunch. In order to get her, I used my grandfather's swiftest running buffalo horse. One morning while the stallion that owned the herd was busy chasing another stallion away, I chased the wild horses and singled this beautiful sorrel out that I had been watching for many moons. I threw a noose over her head. Dismounting, I kept hold of the rope and ran with her until she fell from exhaustion. After I placed hobbles over her feet, and as she struggled I placed my hand over her eyes, and nose. I breathed into her nostrils. This conquered her, and she became mine." Pausing, he sadly said. "I shall miss her." Totally tuckered out and emotionally drained, he threw himself down on the bare floor overcome with despair and grief.

CHAPTER 22

FRIEND OR ENEMY

Frederick was deeply touched at the suffering of his blood brother. He extended his hand to him and pulled him up saying, "Come on brother, let's go out and check on Goldie."

Goldie looked at them in a pious way, and when she saw Ayoka, she made a soft cooing sound. She had lost some feathers in her solo dive. Ayoka picked them up. He could now replace his medicine bag feathers his grandfather had given him with his own feathers. This was his coup. "I do not want to kill her," he said, as he reached over and stroked her head. "Let's untie her brother. Let's see if she is our friend or enemy."

Frederick looked at Goldie cautiously, "Oh, I don't know, Ayoka. I don't know if we should trust her. You untie her. I'll stand over here with my gun, and if she attacks you, I will blow her to feathereens!" Frederick's gun clicked, as he cocked it.

Ayoka quickly untied Goldie's legs. She tried to stand up, but she fell again. Ayoka rubbed her numb legs. Finally she stood up. She lowered her head. Ayoka stroked it. Flapping her huge wings, she flew up towards the peak of Pinnacle Mountain. The great bird of thunder and lightning was quiet as she soared through the air. Ayoka and Frederick watched Goldie as she disappeared through the clouds.

S. BALdwiN

CHAPTER 23

THE SUCCESSFUL HUNT

"We need to hunt for some fresh meat," Ayoka said. It will build our strength up. We don't know how long we will be on this mountain."

"Aho blood brother! Let's get the horses. You can ride Chop Stix. Gypsy is too ornery to let you ride her." Ayoka smiled sadly. He knew a man's horse was his alone.

As they walked towards the gulch they saw many deer tracks. When they arrived at the mouth of the gulch, they saw Gypsy and Chop Stix grazing.

Standing with them was a large buck with a rack of branching horns on his head. He looked so proud, free and wild. There were three does with him.

Placing his index finger on his lips, Frederick mouthed for Ayoka to stand still. He plugged one of the young does in the neck. The other does took up the gulch in leaps and bounds. They watched the magnificent buck bound off into the wilderness. Ayoka ran to the killed deer and with expertise removed the entrails. He threw the doe over his shoulders and mounted Chop Stix, and they rode back to the cave.

The blood brothers dug a hole at the entrance of the cave and built a fire to ward off wild animals. Ayoka skinned the deer giving Wolf his share. He offered Frederick some of the warm uncooked liver. Frederick shook his head in a no answer, and goose bumps ran up and down his spine as Ayoka popped a piece of the raw liver into his mouth eating this delicacy with great pleasure.

Frederick cooked a good piece of the venison on his gun ramrod over the fire for their supper. They drenched the food down with coffee and cornbread. After they filled their bellies, Frederick cleaned his rifle, and loaded it. This would keep them safe. The blood brothers were tired now. It didn't take them long before they were gone to dreamland. It was a quiet night except low growls from Wolf now and then.

C H A P T E R 24

A SIM-A-HI ATTACKS

The next morning Ayoka rose early. The fire had been reduced to ashes. Wolf followed close to Ayoka's heels. When they got outside, in a distance lazy buzzards were circling the sky. Ayoka quickly ran down the path to investigate. There lay Goldie. She was a mass of blood stained bones and feathers. Something had killed her. As he picked up a couple of her prized feathers, he thought, why would she come back? It was unusual for an eagle to return at night.

Ayoka bent down low to the ground looking for prints. The prints were large with five sharp clawed toes imprinted in the sandy soil. "A sim-a-hi (grizzly)!" Ayoka whispered. That was why Goldie had returned; to warn them of the danger. He bowed his head to converse with the spirits. He told them how brave Goldie had been and had been his friend. A strong Chinook wind began blowing. The flapping of wings pulsated the air. The sky grew dark with flocks of eagles. Ayoka shrunk back as they landed and carried the remains of Goldie up towards the heavens with them. Then a cooing whisper like a soft wind blowing said. "Ayoka you have my eagle power now, my inheritance to you for the makings of a great Chief." He knew it was Goldie's spirit.

His feet and legs surged with power like he had never felt before. With the speed of an eagle he sped to the mouth of the cave. He was too late. There stood a massive ten-foot grizzly bear in the center of the cave. This was his cave. He was here to claim it.

Frederick was cornered. His face was ashen. His rifle lay next to his bedroll on the floor. He was backing up slowly. There was no way he could get his gun. The bear weighed about 1000 pounds. His vicious eyes were red, glaring with rage at Frederick. A low continuation of a ferocious growl vibrated throughout the cave.

The hair on Wolf's back bristled like porcupine quills. He pounced through the air, clamping his teeth into the bear's arm. The bear spun around and roared with rage. He wagged his massive head back and forth. With his mighty paws and claws swishing through the air, he knocked Wolf through the cave door. The Grizzly turned back and lumbered towards Frederick.

He had no weapon but he was going to make a smashing blow to the bear's snout. He was so close Frederick could feel his hot, foul stinkin' breath on him. Now Frederick was backed against the cold cave wall. The stubborn streak in him refused to lose hope. His fist doubled, Frederick was ready to fight to the finish. Although petrified, he began yelling insults at the maddened bear.

Just then a loud fearsome yell rang out, "Sim-a-hi!" The bear turned and stomped towards Ayoka, who had his arrow aimed and ready for the kill. He knew if he missed his mark, the bear would become very dangerous, and they would be in serious trouble. With extreme caution, he pulled back the bow. "Twang!" The arrow whizzed through the air piercing the bear's heart. He staggered with a moan, and then clutching his bleeding chest he clawed it, then plunged forward and fell with an enormous thud. Frederick jumped out of the way. But he wasn't quite dead yet. He was uttering low moans and gasping for breath. Blood was flowing out of his wound. The grizzly rolled over and with a thunderous roar and a long sigh his black eyes filmed over with the glaze of death.

Ayoka ran over to him and touched him with his coup stick. At the top of his voice, he screamed, "I've killed you, you stupid red eyed demon. I've given you what you deserved for killing Goldie. The grizzly let out a long sigh and died.

Frederick, his teeth chattering, wiped the sweat from his brow. He was still shaking when Ayoka ran up to him and gave him a powerful hug. In a trembling, voice, Frederick said, "You saved me from becoming bear food, brother. Another coup for you."

Ayoka said, "Hownk! Hownk!" (Means yes, all right, I agree). They hooted with laughter. Getting control of themselves, they said in unison, "Where is Wolf? Ayoka whistled. Wolf, came limping in. The side of his face was bleeding. When he saw the dead bear, he stopped and sat on his haunches and uttered one growl after another.

Later on they cleaned the bear, removing its teeth and front claws. Ayoka said, "When we get back to my camp, there will be two bear teeth and claw necklaces, one for my brother and one for me. These necklaces are a sign of great heroism. You will be a hero when my grandfather hears of our feats. At the powwow he will give you an Indian name." A smile broke over Frederick's face. "Great! Will my name be "Dirty pants?"

CHAPTER 25

SPIRIT OF THE MOUNTAIN

An eerie cackle broke the silence. "Heh, Heh, Heh! Think you are leaving the mountain alive, the only ones to ever do so! Well think again, boys. Your scalps will hang on the peak of Pinnacle Mountain." The cave shook as a hideous laugh echoed throughout the walls.

Ayoka and Frederick looked around. "Who goes there?" Ayoka called shading his eyes, looking towards the walls. Boulders began crashing down from a ledge sending both boys dodging and jumping out of their way.

Holding a torch, the light showed the face and body of a stooped old man with fierce penetrating, squinty eyes, which glowed like burning embers, on a high ledge. His matted gray hair fell below his knees. He held a staff entwined with squirming snakes. He stroked one viper holding its evil head with its flicking tongue up near his face. "My precious ones. You will have a wonderful dinner tonight, my pets. Heh, Heh, Heh!"

The boys shuddered at the sight. Frederick whispered, "That old man must be 100 years old."

Ayoka replied, "He is the 'Spirit of the Mountain'. Ayoka raised his left arm in a gesture of peace, saying, "Old spirit man, we have not come to harm anyone." We just came to explore the mountain. We want nothing from you."

In a sharp tongued voice, he said, "Quiet, Injun. You know of the Pinnacle's treasure. That is what you are after! And you killed my pet bear."

"Well it was either your pet bear or us!" Frederick called out.

"Don't be insolent with me boy. You're not Injun. Who are you?"

"That's for me to know and you to find out." Frederick shouted.

The old man slowly came down from the ledge and stood in front of Frederick, leering at him. "Boy you're too free with that tongue of yours." Lifting the staff he put the snake's squirming head in his face. Frederick's with an astonished look jerked his head back. The old man laughed showing his yellowed and jagged teeth. "You're afeared aren't you boy?"

In a fit of anger, Frederick whipped his knife from its sheath, grabbed the snake from the old man's hand and whacked its head off, slamming it to the floor. Headless, it wiggled across the floor. The old man's face became red and twisted in rage. He raised the staff and swung it towards Frederick. Frederick ducked.

Ayoka stood looking aghast at Frederick. His blood brother had the agility of a fox and the bravery of the gods. Coming up behind him, Ayoka grabbed the old man in an iron grasp lifting him off the ground. The staff rolled across the cave floor. The man's feet and arms danced wildly about in the air.

Frederick called, "Ayoka, keep your hold on this spirit man. The ornery old man is strong as an ox." Quickly Frederick tied his hands together behind his back, as Ayoka held him. Then he shackled his feet. They were breathless when they finished wrestling with this wild man. They propped him up against a big stone slab.

Ayoka said "This man (pant, pant) might be ancient, but he has great strength."

"Yeah, Old Spirit man," Frederick said, "now where is the snake pit you were going to put us in? Wolf, guard him, and make him mind his manners!"

With a sly suspicious look, the old man began moving his head and neck back and forth. An amulet was hanging by a chain around his wrinkled, leathery neck. In the center of the stone was a brilliant, light flashing, skeleton figurine. Ayoka stared at its swinging motion. Back and forth it swung. The old man said in a low antagonistic, quavering voice not wanting Frederick to hear him, "Go up on the ledge and follow the path through the tunnel. That's where the treasure lies Injun."

Frederick had walked over and stoked the fire to warm the coffee. Turning around, he saw Ayoka staring at the spirit man. "Ayoka, have a cup of this coffee," he said, as he began pouring some in a cup.

Ayoka did not respond. Instead he turned and walking like a zombie headed for the cave stairs. Frederick realized that Ayoka was in a hypnotic trance-like state. That amulet around the spirit man's neck had put Ayoka under its spell. The spirit man had a sly sneer on his face.

Quickly Frederick ran over to the old man and yanked the chain from his neck, shoving it in his pocket. "You can not be trusted, old man. We'll find the treasure, and then we will take your scalp for another coup, and throw your body in the snake pit." He ran over to the stairs and began shaking Ayoka vigorously. This snapped a bewildered Ayoka out of his numbed state. "Sorry brother," Frederick said.

The old man cowered down, saying, "Give me back my charm, you insolent boy."

Taking it from his pocket, Frederick slammed it against the stone wall. "So much for your magic charm Spirit man." The glass splintered into pieces. Rising from the broken debris was an eerie skeleton, with a hellish laugh, which echoed throughout the cave disappearing in a black mist.

CHAPTER 26

❀

PASSAGE OF DOOM

Frederick rubbed his chin, thinking. You're too eager for us to find the treasure, old Spirit man. Let's take him with us Ayoka. He can lead us to whatever he is worried about."

With a look of terror, and his voice shaking with fear, the old man began talking fast, "No, No, I'm too weak. I need to rest. You don't need my help. You'll find it without me. A splennnnnnndid treasure."

"Get up, old man! Lead us to the treasure. Now!" Frederick jerked him to his feet.

Ayoka cut the rope from the old man's hands and feet and handed him his walking staff. "Wolf keep Whiskers moving." Wolf nipped his butt. The old man moved at a quicker pace. When they got to the ledge, 'The Spirit man balked at going through the tunnel.

"You boys go first. The treasure is straight ahead," he muttered.

"Move old Spirit man," Frederick said. "You get the honors of going first."

Wolf growled and nipped him on the butt again.

"Call that dang mutt off me," the old man growled. Slowly he led them down a twisted tunnel-like dusty passage poking his staff in the floor ahead of him. Chuckling he said, "Warnin' the rattlers to git out our way." Then he bent his head down low.

Frederick stopped in his tracks. "What do you mean rattlers?"

Ayoka said as he brushed past him, "Let me stay behind the old man. Keep your head down low Frederick."

He stubbornly answered, "There's enough head room for us to stand straight. We're not decrypted yet. Bad for the back."

"You talk too much brother. Bats are on the ceiling wall. If you brush against the ceiling, you'll have hundred's swooping down on us. And we sure as shootin' don't want bats tangled in our hair."

Frederick pulled his hat over his ears.

The cave walls were lined with flickering torches. Ayoka pointed to human bones and skulls in heaping piles along the way. "So this is what happened to our Indian braves." Ayoka shook his head in disbelief. "Did you kill those braves old man?"

"They were after the Pinnacle's treasure. I let most of them starve or fed them to the snakes. Nobody leaves my mountain!" The old man turned around and peered at them with an evil grin spread across his grimy, whiskered face.

CHAPTER 27

TOO LATE TO TURN BACK

As they walked along the narrow ledge through the dimly lit tunnel, Ayoka pointed at the walls, which were covered with inscriptions and carvings. They were creepy carvings, all depicting skeletons killing men.

Ayoka said, "These walls are cursed." Drum throbbing became intense, and weird chants reverberated throughout the cave. Ayoka and Frederick exchanged terrified looks. "Maybe we had better turn back Frederick. This looks like a passage to the evil spirits of the netherworld."

Frederick shuddered. "If it is, we will be trapped forever. But we've come this far Ayoka. We can't quit now!"

Ayoka nodded his head in agreement. His blood brother was a brave one, but a little on the stupid side. Walking on, they came to a dead-end blocked by an enormous boulder. A huge skull with gold nuggets for the eyes and a large ruby for the nose was embedded in the stone with the writing of "Beware" beneath it. The drum noise increased its tempo. Ayoka said, "We're cave-blocked, "We either go in or turn back."

Turning to look back where they had come from, Frederick shook his head and said, "Too late Ayoka. Look!"

Ayoka turned and looked. There was no way they could go back. A solid wall from nowhere had risen behind them. It was now a no-way path. The mountain seemed to be closing around them. They were trapped. There was no place to go. "Well what do we do now, great Paleface?"

"Old Spirit man of the Mountain, you knew this would happen. That's why you wanted to lag behind. It's a good thing we made you the leader. You could escape before the wall appeared, and we would have been crushed." Watching the wall slowly sliding up towards them, Frederick didn't hesitate. "We're going in." Desperately he began trying to roll the boulder aside. "Old man help us push this open."

The old man's eyes were full of alarm, as he said; "It won't open. You can push all you want to, but it still won't open. It's too late. We'll be squashed like buffalo chips, but it's best to be killed this way." The old man grabbed at his chest.

Ayoka said, "Old man you speak with a forked tongue." He stepped beside the boulder and began pushing with Frederick pulling the other side. The wall behind them was slowly crowding them against the boulder. They heaved and shoved on the boulder again. It would not budge.

"Dadburn it, I told you, that it can't be opened," the old man muttered. They were now bunched together. They could barely move. Soon the wall would smash them like pancakes. The air was hot and low in oxygen. It was hard to breathe. Time was running out for all of them.

Frederick lost his patience. He drew back his arm with his fist doubled. "Take this," he yelled. He punched the skull in its jeweled nose. The boulder slowly slid open. Frederick couldn't believe his eyes."

"Yeah!" Ayoka yelled jubilantly, "See Frederick, your bad temper saved us."

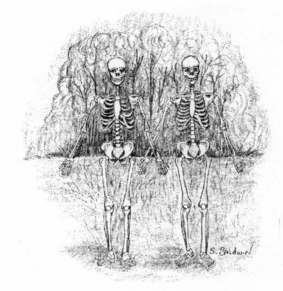

CHAPTER 28

THE SECRET OF PINNACLE UNFOLDS

Ayoka pushed the old man in first. Frederick and he shielded their eyes because of the brilliant radiance of gold and silver studded walls covered with nuggets blinded them. The cave ceiling was sprinkled with diamonds twinkling like stars in the heavens. There were shimmering icicle formations hanging from the ceiling. It was a netherworld of awesome beauty unfolding before their eyes. Glittering white gypsum chandeliers hung from the ceiling. The wonders of the cavern were so enchanting that the two of them forgot about the old man.

"Aiiiiiiieeeeee!" The old man let out a blood-curdling scream. He was being drug into a circle of unearthly, weird ghost-like skeletons, moving slowly, chanting and beating drums. It was a scene never to be forgotten. With all of the room's beauty, evil surrounded them.

"Look," Ayoka whispered. "They all have those chains around their necks."

Frederick said, "Whatever you do don't look at any of those charms."

The old man was thrust in front of a tall skeleton with a crown of horns on his head. His eyes were deep black chambers, having no end to their depth.

In a ghostly voice, he said, "Spirit man of the Mountain, you have brought strangers in, letting them know the secret of Pinnacle. You shall pay the consequences."

"This is the cave of the living dead," Frederick whispered. He was dead serious.

"No, no, Great Chief," The old man screamed. There was a hysterical note of alarm in his voice. He dropped to the floor, throwing his arms around the skeleton's feet. The monstrous skeleton kicked the old man, knocking out two of his jagged teeth. Then with his long spindly finger, he pointed to two spear holding skeletons. In an eerie and frightening voice he screamed, "Kill him. We'll drink his blood!"

A mist of evil filled the cavern. One skeleton speared the old man's body with the wound gushing blood like a fountain and flung him into a swirling, smoldering pool filled with snakes. With a shrill nightmarish scream, the undercurrent of the thirsty water swallowed him. Now the pool was filled with bubbling blood and snakes began to thrash about and fight each other. The skeletons crowded around watching the scene with great relish, their white tongues licking the drools from their mouths. One skeleton, his bones clanking, removed a big dipper from a pyramid stand of glistening white stone, which rose up from the floor. He dipped it into the pool of blood, filling a silver goblet to the brim. He handed it to their chief who gulped it down, turning his white bones into red bones. "Ahhhhh," he moaned. "More!"

"The river of blood from my vision!" Ayoka whispered.

Frederick yelled at the top of his lungs, "Hey! Let's get out of here." There was alarm in his voice. They turned to flee, but a wall stood where the bolder opening had been. There was no escape.

HANG THEIR SCALPS ON PINNACLE PEAK

The skeletons grabbed Ayoka and Frederick, dragging them up to their Leader. They stood facing the hideous skeleton leader eye to eye. He placed his long spindly fingers on their shoulders, turning them around to face his skeleton subjects. Pointing at them with a long bony finger, he said, "These outsiders, dared to tread on sacred ground. No one leaves Pinnacle Mountain alive. What shall we do with them, my subjects?"

The skeletons yelled in unison. Their bones clattered noisily. "Kill them. Kill them. Hang their scalps on top of Pinnacle Mountain."

Ayoka, with beads of sweat rolling down his face, grabbed Frederick's hand, squeezing it tightly. "Be brave brother of mine. We will die together and meet at the Happy Hunting Ground." Then he closed his eyes tightly and began singing the death chant.

Frederick, the veins standing out in his neck, flinched. He broke away from the skeleton leader jumping up on a high rock. Holding up his doubled fists, he shouted, "Not without a fight Ayoka! Let's whip these Boneheads. Stop singing that weird chant!"

Ayoka jerked away from his captors. Both of the boys began hand to hand combat, punching and kicking the bony skeletons, but it was useless. They were unable to hurt them.

CHAPTER 30

HELP IS ON THE WAY

Suddenly the ground began to shake and crumble. An ear splitting thunderous sound echoed throughout the chamber. A pyramid of glistening alabaster rose up from the floor. The boys jumped on it. While everything else was crumbling, this rock stood solid. Instead of feeling exhausted, the boys were full of new energy. A loud bellowing roar echoed through the room. The skeletons danced uncontrollably, falling against the wall.

With extraordinary speed, a herd of white buffalo came crashing through the cave. Leading the herd was a huge white buffalo bull. Frederick shouted, "Ayoka that's the buffalo that appeared at our ranch."

Ayoka said, "And that's the same buffalo of my vision. That is my Protector!"

Fire flashed from the white bull's nostrils and his snorting deafened their ears, echoing and re-echoing throughout the cave.

Ayoka yelled, "This is it brother; Good-bye!"

Frederick stood speechless and spellbound. His chest felt tight with raw fear.

A booming voice deep and haunting, roared, "It's not a good time to die, Ayoka. You must leave Pinnacle Mountain now, and never return. You have proved your bravery and have conquered the mountain!" The White Bull knelt down and bellowed louder, "Jump and mount me, both of you!"

"Hallelujah!" Frederick shouted. "Let's scram!"

Wasting no time, Ayoka grabbed Frederick's hand and together they jumped on the bull's back. Ayoka held on to his huge horns. Frederick wrapped his arms around Ayoka. They zoomed through the skeleton bones that were sprawled out all over the cave floor. Thinking that the cave cavity did not have an opening, both Frederick and Ayoka closed their eyes tightly ready for a crash, but the icicle formations opened as they raced through to the fresh air of freedom. The formations closed the exit completely as they headed down the mountain. Out of nowhere Chop Stix, Gypsy and Wolf appeared following close behind. Shrieks and screams could be heard for miles. The white bull's herds of buffalo were demolishing the skeletons and their cave of doom. The skeleton band and their leader were perishing under hooves of the maddened herd. The secret of Pinnacle was safe forever.

The White Bull galloped at a frightful speed and did not stop until they were at the base of the mountain on the plains. He came to an abrupt halt and Ayoka and Frederick both sailed over the bull's head and hit the ground landing in front of him. They were so stunned they could not move. The White Bull looked at them saying, "Take the secret of Pinnacle Mountain to your grave." He then shook his noble head and trotted off, disappearing in the evening gray mist.

Under his horns they could have been gored. Ayoka looked at Frederick. "He saved our lives. I shall ever be grateful to my protector."

"Whew, you can say that again," Frederick said as he wiped sweat from his brow.

Clasping their hands together into one hardened fist and raising their lean and muscular arms up towards the sky they shouted together, "blood brothers Forever!"

Ayoka said, "My blood brother, it's time to return to my grandfather's lodge and tell him of our adventure. I want you to come with me. There will be a big celebration, and my tribe will want to meet my brother who saved my life many times.

Frederick put his hand on his heart, "My heart is filled with love for my brother who saved my life many times, but it is time for me to leave for my home. Pa and Wee will be worried."

Ayoka's voice became somber. "I understand brother, but give me your word you will come to our camp soon, so we can celebrate. You have many coups, and you have earned an Indian name which my grandfather will give to you." He squeezed Frederick's hand hard. "When I get back to camp I will send a messenger to your house telling you when to come."

Chop Stix, Gypsy and Wolf were frolicking through the prairie grass unaware of the emotional moment. They had been through many terrorizing moments together. Gypsy was nuzzling Chop Stix's neck. They had become more than fast friends.

Frederick called Chop Stix. He pranced over, his mischievous eyes flashing. Wolf came running too, rubbing his cold nose against Frederick's arm. "Chop Stix you are my gift to Ayoka. My little mule has proven himself to be very brave on our perilous journey. He will be a good friend to you Ayoka." Then he stooped down and petted Wolf. "I'll miss you Wolf." Looking at Ayoka, he said, "I have a new name for brave Wolf. It's 'Most Lordly Dog.'" Wolf, his tongue hanging out, wagged his tail. He was a very happy 'Most Lordly Dog'.

"Look," Ayoka called, as he pointed off to a high cliff. "It's my great Protector." When Ayoka looked back at Frederick, he was gone.

Frederick galloped away at high speed, leaving whirls of dust. He held his hat high in the air, not looking back. He never did like good-byes.

CHAPTER 31

HOME AGAIN

It was dusk when Frederick saw the ranch in the distance. They had ridden hard, so hard that sweat lathered Gypsy's mouth. Frederick led Gypsy into the barn, giving her oats and water. While she was filling her belly, he brushed and wiped her down with a soft cloth until her coat shined. "You're on your own now, Gypsy." He rushed towards the cabin and burst through the door.

His dad was sitting at the table. When he saw Frederick, he jumped up and grabbed him. "Son, you're finally home. Sit down. I'll fix you something to eat."

Where's Wee Pa?" Frederick asked, looking around.

"She left a few days ago. She went to visit her grandfather. She missed you very much. No telling when she'll be back. Soon I hope, but she has lots to tell her relatives and friends."

Frederick noticed hesitancy in his dad's voice. He had something on his mind. Is something troubling you Pa?"

Big Otto rose from his chair, and walked over to Frederick. He placed his hands on his shoulders. In a solemn voice he said, "You could always read my mind, Son." Raking his hand through his hair, he continued, "Yes my son, I have something special to tell you. I don't know how you are going to take it."

Frederick turned looking at him. He had never seen him like this. "What is it Pa? I can take it. Since I have been gone, I have had to take on responsibilities that only a man could take on. I didn't have you around to rely on. Pa, I am a man!" With that statement, Frederick got up from his chair, and placed his hands on his dad's shoulders. Looking his Pa in the eyes, he said in a firm voice, "You can tell me anything, Pa. Good or bad!"

Otto eyed his son with a new respect. "Son, I believe you're right. You have grown into a man whom I am very proud of. Sit back down son. This will take some time." Walking over to the stove, he poured Frederick and him a cup of hot coffee. Looking serious and thoughtful he began talking.

"When you left that morning for Pinnacle, I never saw Wee express such emotion since she has lived with us. We walked back into the cabin after you left, and sometime after we went to bed, I heard a sobbing coming from her bedroom. I got up and listened. Knocking softly on her door, I called to her. I waited a few minutes, then the door opened, and in the moonlight filled room, there was this most beautiful, childlike creature standing there, with her hands covering her eyes, sobbing. I slowly removed her hands, and those glistening blue eyes were filled with tears, streaming down her cheeks like a waterfall. I lifted her in my arms, and carried her over to the rocking chair by the window." He paused. "You know son, the rocking chair we brought from Germany that belonged to your Mama?" Frederick nodded. "I rocked her in my arms, kissing the tears away, and singing softly to her until morning. She fell asleep, and I gently laid her onto her bed."

Frederick's eyes were moist. "You don't have to go on Pa."

"No son, I want to finish. That morning, I fixed her breakfast. Then I professed my love for her and asked her if I was good enough to be her husband. You won't believe it son, but she grabbed me, kissing and hugging me, saying, "I would be honored to be the wife of Big Otto and a mother to his son Frederick. But why have you waited so long to ask?"

I was stunned but I yelled "Yahoo!" I couldn't believe my luck. This beautiful woman wanted to be my wife all this time, and I was so blind." But then we both looked at each other, saying together. "What will Frederick say, and how will he feel about this union?"

Frederick jumped up from his chair. "Oh Pa, this puts the icing on the cake. You and Wee married? Pa, Ayoka will not only be a blood brother, but my uncle too!"

"But this is great. You really mean it son? Everything is okay?" Otto was grinning from ear to ear.

A loud knock on the cabin door interrupted their conversation. Otto hollered, "Since when do you knock? Come in Jake and look who's here."

Jake stormed in giving Frederick a whack on the back. "Bout time you came back Frederick. Thought we'd have to come git you!"

Otto said, "You're just in time to hear about his adventure. "Tell us about your trip to Pinnacle and your meeting Ayoka, son." They all sat down with cups of steaming coffee and some sugar cookies that Wee had made before she left.

Jake reached over and grabbed Frederick's hand. "What in the tarnation did you do to those knuckles."

Frederick looked down at his hand. Knowing that he couldn't lie to Unk Jake or to anybody for that matter, he said, "Oh, I knocked it against a big rock, Unk."

Big Jake said, "Bull!"

Fred told them about most of the adventure, but remembering what the white bull had said, he left the secret of Pinnacle out. They talked until the early wee hours in the morning.

CHAPTER 32

WEE'S RETURN

The aroma of sizzling bacon found its way throughout the cabin. Big Otto woke with a start. The sunlight was so bright that he shielded his eyes upon opening them. In a stupor he rubbed his eyes, then he jumped out of bed. The bright sun told him it was beyond early morning. Running to the water basin, he splashed water over his whiskered face. Quickly he dressed and shaved. Then he heard a light knock at his door. Opening it, there stood Wee. He grabbed her small waist, with his huge hands, lifting her into the air and twirling her around the room. She held on tightly, giggling softly.

"You're home. The love of my life has returned." He put her down. She grabbed his hand, pulling him into the kitchen.

"You sleepyhead. It's almost noon, and your chores haven't been touched. We need wood and water. But first your breakfast is ready and waiting."

"Where's Jake? He was here when I went to bed last night."

"He left early this morning. I fixed him some breakfast. Said he had lots to catch up on at his den."

Otto thought, she doesn't know. I won't tell her. She served his favorite breakfast of cornmeal pancakes with honey syrup, bacon, eggs and her fluffy biscuits with milk gravy. Topping this meal were blueberries she had picked along the way home from her trip. Rubbing his stomach, Otto said, "Wee this breakfast is fit for a king. What's the occasion?"

She looked at him saying. You are my king, and I will be your slave forever."

Otto looked at her and said, "Haven't you heard? Palefaces are slaves to their women? You are my princess."

She blushed demurely, and sat down, and lowered her eyes in prayer.

As they prayed, Frederick sneaked in, and at the end of the prayer, he placed his hands over her eyes. She twisted around in her chair, saying, "Welcome home, our Frederick."

Frederick looked at her in surprise. "How did you know I was back Wee?"

"I was in the Black Hills when Ayoka returned. He told us all about your dangerous adventure and your bravery, how you saved him, how you..." Then she covered her eyes saying, "Oh Otto, our braves almost didn't get back."

"Whoa, Ayoka has a big mouth. It was the other way around. Your brother is very brave and noble. Someday he will make a great chief of the Sioux tribe." He pulled Wee up from her chair and holding her tightly said, "But you and pa are the big news. There's going to be a wedding, I understand."

"Oh, Otto told you. Is it okay Frederick?"

His face was ablaze with happiness. "You know it is, but you're too young to be my mother." He hugged her. "The news made my heart happy."

"Sit down and eat. I rushed home, so I could have your favorite breakfast ready."

Frederick sat down and spooned the gravy onto the fluffy biscuits. "It's good being back. This is the best meal I've had since I left."

After satisfying his appetite, Frederick went to his room and brought back a pouch. He walked over to Wee and said, "Ayoka and I brought this back for you." He handed it to her. She carefully opened it.

"Bear teeth! Grizzly bear teeth! Oh Frederick, you and Ayoka were so brave. She looked at him sweetly. "He told me about the Sim-i-la. I shall make a bear necklace for both of my young braves."

His face reddened as he handed her another larger bag. In it were the bear's claws. "You can make your self some earrings and a necklace with these."

Wee threw her arms around him, laying her head against his chest. "Oh Frederick, an early wedding present. I shall make a necklace to wear on my wedding day."

Frederick's neck and face grew flushed. "Come on Pa. It's time to do the chores." Big Otto grinned.

CHAPTER 33

WHERE THERE'S SMOKE, THERE'S FIRE

Chopping word was an early morning chore, but getting started late, they worked up a sweat in the hot afternoon sun. After filling the woodbin in the cabin with several armfuls of wood, they were more than anxious to go to the creek for water. Holding buckets they raced each other to the creek. They both dove in, clothes and all.

"Look, Pa." Frederick pointed towards the Black Hills. Smoke was curling through the air, making puffs now and then. "Those are smoke signals coming out of the Black Hills."

Otto shaded his hands over his eyes looking towards the Black Hills. Faint throbs of beating drums could be heard. "Wonder what is going on with the Indians. Hope they are not preparing for war."

"War?" Ayoka asked with a startled look. "Why would they want war?"

"Well the government knows there is gold in the Black Hills, and word has spread throughout the country. People are coming to the plains in droves and trespassing on Indian Territory. Chief Big Horn and his people are not happy about this disturbance of their land, and they have started attacking the wagon trains and gold rushers."

"War would be a terrible thing, Pa. I could never fight the Indians, and I could never let my country down neither. This land belonged to the Indians before the white man came along. Ayoka and I against each other? Never!" The thought of an ugly war made his eyes fierce with anger. "But they aren't bothering the Black Hills, are they Pa?" Frederick's forehead was wrinkled with worry. "Ayoka told me that Chief Big Horn and Yellow Hair had a treaty, that the Black Hills were sacred and belonged to the Sioux Indians."

"So far the government has promised that the Black Hills of the Dakota country would be untouched, son. It's one of the prettiest lands on the prairie. There's scenic beauty with deep canyons, and towering rugged rock formations. It has a deep wilderness of pine and spruce forests. People realize that the Black Hills are rich with minerals, gold, clay and sand." Otto paused looking towards the Black Hills. "Yep, it's a Pandora's box full of treasurers, and the Indians will fight until their death to keep it."

Frederick said, "I hope they won't have to Pa." They trudged back and forth from the creek with filled pails of water. Frederick tended to the sheep and the horses, while his dad milked the cow. It was almost evening, and they were still not finished working.

The anvil clanged. It was time for supper. Dark clouds formed in the sky. There was still much to do before the rains began. The Chinook (winds) began to rattle the tin barn roof, and a sudden downpour began. They high tailed it to the cabin.

Their supper had been put on the stove keeping it warm. Wee was working diligently by the flickering light of the oil lamp. She covered whatever she was doing when Frederick and Otto kissed her on the cheek and bid her "good night."

The torrential rain beat against the windows all night. The thunder roared and echoed throughout the prairie like herds of stampeding buffalo. Flashes of lightning zigzagged across Frederick's darkened room. The orchestrated storm had a lulling effect on him. It felt so good to be in his soft feather bed again.

CHAPTER 34

THE MESSENGER

Frederick woke up to a deafening silence. He looked out of his dimpled dust covered window. It had stopped raining. The plains had sucked the welcomed water into its murky depths. This was Frederick's favorite time of the day. He dressed quietly and softly tiptoed barefoot out of the cabin.

As he dreamily looked at the sky, a beautiful fluorescent rainbow appeared. He made a wish as he always did, always wondering what was at the end of the rainbow. The restlessness and adventurous spirit of his never ceased.

Grabbing his cane-fishing pole from the porch he skipped down the steps toward the creek. The never-ending plains rose up to meet the sky. How small he felt. He never got use to the vastness of the plains. Everything was fresh and new in the mornings. The scent of the storm was still in the air. His heart swelled as his eyes drank in the beauty of the land. The cottonwoods bordering the creek with their thirsty roots stretching into the water were overwhelming. The honking of a v-shape formation of geese flying overhead interrupted the tranquillity of the morning.

Frederick stood at the creek's edge under the shade of the cottonwood trees. He cast his fishing line into the water watching the circles the penetrating hook had made. It wasn't long until his hook started to bobble then a slight jerk. A quick yank brought a shimmering whitefish out of the water, then another one, then another one, until he had a string of fish. Wee will be happy to have fish for supper tonight, he thought.

By now the sun had come up, beating down its hot rays on the sandy bank. The water was inviting. Taking his string of fish, he hung them on a clump of roots by the water. Then looping his clothes over one of the swaying cotton-wood branches he plunged into the water with a big splash. Squinting he caught sight of something moving in the tall grass. He ducked his head under the water.

Frederick hadn't brought his gun. He said to himself, I'm in big trouble. Unk Jake had warned him never to go anywhere without his gun. But then, second-guessing himself, he thought, it's probably a deer moving through the brush. Just then a lazy turtle slid off a log into the water with a splash. Frederick said, "Whew!"

An earsplitting "Whoop" broke the silence startling him, and out rode an Indian in all of his full regalia dress. Wheeling his pinto pony up in the air, he raised his lance, and in a commanding voice said, "Tac Ha na dah pe (Come here!)."

Frederick didn't have a stitch of clothes on. In fact, he just had his birthday suit on. He ducked in deeper water with only his head showing. He quickly said in Indian tongue, "Peace Brother. I do not have any clothes on. If you are a fair brave looking for a skirmish, at least give me a fighting chance, and hand me my clothes."

The Indian was surprised when Ayoka spoke in his tongue, and a slight smile played over his lips. "Me Bold One." He pointed to himself. "Me not here to harm you. Ayoka sent me. Chief Big Horn is giving powwow in your and Ayoka's honor. You and your family come!"

Wading towards the shore as far as he dared, with a relieved look on his face, Frederick said, "When? Where?"

The Indian raised his lance pointing towards the Black Hills. "Come when the drums stop beating." Wheeling his horse around to leave, he suddenly stopped, swooped down and grabbed the string of fish. "Me take Oh hong (fish) back to camp, gift to Chief Big Horn from you. Make him feel good." Then he left.

Frederick chuckled and said aloud, "Who am I to argue with a lance wielding Indian!" He quickly dressed and went back to the cabin.

Wee was sweeping the cabin floor, and Big Otto was sitting at the table watching her. "Sit down for a spell Wee," Frederick said, as he pulled out a chair for her. I meant to be back sooner, but I had an unexpected visitor while swimming."

CHAPTER 35

THE JOURNEY

When he told them about the visit, Wee said she knew there was going to be a big celebration, but wasn't quite sure when it would happen. Wee explained that when they went to visit, they might be there for awhile, because when there were powwows, they lasted for several days. Otto asked Jake if he would mind taking care of the animals and crops while they were gone.

You could see the excitement and happiness in Wee's face about the coming event. From that day on, the kitchen smelled of baking and food preparation. At night Wee stayed up late working on someone's gift for the powwow, but she was very secretive about it.

Wee mentioned to Otto that she needed some supplies from the trading post in the nearby town of Boonesville.

Otto said, "We'll leave when the sun rises. I need some things too."

Frederick was excited about going, as they always had lots of fun browsing through the small town of Boonesville. It was three hours away.

Early the next morning, they woke up to a breakfast of hot cakes and syrup. Otto had already hitched the horses to the clapboard wagon. After breakfast they climbed into the wagon and moved out at a steady pace. Wee was anxious to go too, because she wanted to buy some brown calico to make a skirt for her trip and get gifts to take with her to her friends. While she shopped, Otto knew the storekeeper, Mr. Lantz, and he would enjoy visiting with his friends around the pot-bellied stove. He would even play checkers on the barrel-made table while he was there.

On the way they noticed several soldiers on horseback in an orderly formation in the hills overlooking the prairie. Several canvas-covered wagons drawn by oxen rolled westward over the Oregon Trail with new people coming to make homesteads.

Wee shaded her hands, waving, as she observed them. "I hope they don't tread in the sacred Black Hills. There will be trouble if they do."

Otto put his arm around her saying, "Don't worry your pretty little head about those matters, Wee. You have enough to do with our weddin' comin' up."

She giggled and cuddled up close to him. She could not help but worry about the future of her people.

Soon the frontier town of Boonesville came into view. It boasted a main street as wide as a field, allowing plenty of room for teams and wagons to travel at a comfortable pace. Otto stopped the horses in front of Lance's General Store, so Wee could walk up the steps to the raised wooden sidewalks and begin shopping. The wooden sidewalks were a big help keeping the customer's feet above the mud and dust of the street.

While Wee shopped, Frederick and Otto went to the livery stable and blacksmith's shop. The horses had to be looked at making sure their feet were shod all right, and watered. Arm in arm father and son walked back to the general store. Wee chatted with some women while Mrs. Lantz measured some fabric for her. The store was crammed with merchandise.

Frederick grabbed a pickle from the pickle barrel, and Otto looked at the plows and talked to Jim. Frederick eyed the peppermint balls that were gaily displayed in huge glass jars. Gypsy and Chop Stix liked these tasteful little candies too, so he bought a pocket full. After making their purchases and visiting for a spell, Otto looked at the clock on the wall said, "Come on, we need to git home before nighttime."

CHAPTER 36

THE DRUMS STOPPED BEATING

One morning when they awoke, the never-ending sounds of the Indian drums were silent. The time had arrived for them to leave on their journey to the Black Hills. Wee explained to Otto and Frederick that the beating of the drum was very important, because it brought people together and represented the heartbeat of the Indian nation.

Wee had packed almost everything needed for the trip. "We must leave as soon as possible. Chief Big Horn is expecting us."

"Blue Eyes, you've had everything packed for days. Why don't we head out in the morning at daybreak?' Otto was eager to get the trip behind them.

"Oh Otto, I was hoping you would say that." Her eyes shown with delight.

Jake arrived that night at suppertime. He said he would spend the night in the hayloft in the barn. While Wee cleaned up the evening dishes, Otto, Frederick and Jake sat up late into the night talking about Jake's adventures with the Indians and the wild animals of the plains. "Unk, do you want me to bring anything back for you?" Frederick asked.

Jake just laughed and said, "Maybe one of those pretty Injuns maidens."

Big Otto and Frederick rose early the next morning. Jake was already up and ate breakfast with them. They ate in a hurry and headed out to finish loading the travois with clothing, gifts, and food for friends and relatives. Otto had bought Wee a splendid reddish spotted pinto pony to go on the trip, pulling her travois. She was a well-behaved pony. Wee called her 'Baby'.

Otto and his spirited Bay horse pranced gingerly over to Wee's side. His eyes scanned her. How lovely she looked in her dark brown calico outfit. Her legs had deerskin boots on that he had bought her from the trading post. On the hem of her dress she had stitched beadwork. She surely was his princess. Her slim bronze colored arms held the bridle to the splendid spotted pinto pony he had bought her. She had tied a feather to Baby's bridle, to help him have the speed of the wind. Their eyes met. He whispered, "How beautiful you are." Her olive cheeks blushed a light peach, and she lowered her exquisite blue eyes, her long lashes sweeping her face.

Frederick mounted Gypsy and let the horse have her head. Frederick enjoyed the smooth action under him and raced ahead on Gypsy on the freedom of the plains. He was eager to see his blood brother again.

Otto had decided on a meeting place for lunch. When the sun was straight up in the sky Frederick arrived at their destination. It was by the river where a clump of willow trees stood. Gypsy and Frederick were both thirsty. Wee and Pa got there shortly after. Wee spread a muslin tablecloth on a grassy knoll under the shade of the trees. She had fixed a cold luncheon of turkey sandwiches on fresh baked bread and a big jug of lemonade. For dessert, she had fixed their favorite sugar cookies. As soon as the filling food was eaten, they began their journey again.

They watched prairie schooners rolling bumpily along The Oregon Trail. Shaking his head sadly, Otto said, "Those poor devils. They should have started earlier so they could have been settled for spring planting time to have food for winter. Life sure will be rugged for them for awhile."

Frederick raced ahead and cantered Gypsy to the top of a bluff from where his eyes could see down the prairie. The sun was dropping fast below the shadowy Black Hills in the distance. Frederick drew Gypsy to a stop and dismounted. His eyes took a lingering gaze at the beauty of the landscape. His heart swelled looking at the splendor of the Black Hills in the distance with their mountains towering above the flat prairie. Great rock formations formed into unusual forms. He couldn't help but wonder what lay beyond this tremendous land. Some day he aimed to find out. He searched in his pockets and pulled out two peppermint balls, one for him and one for Gypsy. He rubbed the horse's neck affectionately. "Here I brought one of your favorite candies for our trip because this is a special time in our lives, isn't it?" Then he popped one into his mouth and quickly mounted his beloved horse. On one of the distant hills Frederick saw a rider on a mule holding a staff. Frederick shaded his eyes. He dug his heels lightly into Gypsy's sides and dashed down to the flat prairie. "Ayoka, my brother!" The echo vibrated softly, "Ayoka, my brotherrrrrr!" He gave Gypsy full rein and lit out at a quickened speed to meet his comrades.

The mule brayed loudly, "Heehaw, Heehaw." Lickety-split the mule and rider came down the hill onto the plains. A white streak was leading them. It was Wolf, the 'Most Lordliest dog'! Running at full speed, Wolf jumped through the air into Frederick's opened arms. Trying to keep on his horse by hugging Gypsy tightly with his legs, Frederick lost his balance. He and Wolf went flying through the air landing on the prickly ground. Wolf was overcome with joy swishing his wet, rough tongue all over Frederick's face.

Ayoka jumped off of Chop Stix and pulled Frederick up from the ground. They embraced each other, both talking at once. Chop Stix and Gypsy were nuzzling each other. Looking at Gypsy, Ayoka said, "Looks like you've been feeding her too many oats Frederick. She's getting fat!"

"Fredrick patted Gypsy gently. "She has a good reason to be fat." Frederick grinned. "Chop Stix is going to be a father soon Ayoka."

Ayoka slapped Chop Stix on the fanny, "You old rascal you!" Then he quickly mounted Chop Stix again, and called back to Frederick, "I'll race you to my village."

Frederick climbed on Gypsy, calling; "You're not playing fair. You're ahead already. Besides I need to be easy with Gypsy!"

"Harte, Har, Har," laughed Ayoka. Chop Stix brayed.

Wee and Otto lagged behind looking at the sun setting, as lovers do.

THE ARRIVAL

It was not long before they arrived at a large Indian camp located on the Big Missouri River surrounded by willow trees. There was a huge circle with one opening of cone-shaped teepees set majestically against the level landscape.

As they entered the village, Wee pointed to one very large teepee with artistic drawings on it. Several horses were tethered behind it. Wealth was measured in the number of horses an Indian owned. "This is my grandfather's lodge," she proudly said.

Frederick and Big Otto were impressed with the many horses the Chief had. He was certainly very rich with honor. Wee explained that he was generous and had given many horses away also. Their grandfather had always taught Ayoka and Wee that it was fine being a good warrior, but it was more important to be a generous and giving member of the tribe. This was always hard for Ayoka to understand, but his grandfather set a good example for all that knew him.

The camp was abuzz with happy excitement. This was a time of rejoicing, fun, feasting and visiting with old friends. Some of the women were busy drying meat and beading exquisite moccasins. Some were making arrows. Indian children were running throughout the area. Some were walking on stilts, and the smaller children were riding wooden stick horses. The babies were in cradleboards, laughing and cooing as they watched the older children at play. An old woman greeted Wee handing her a pair of white beaded moccasins. Then she led Wee to a majestic teepee. "Home while you visit us," she said with a merry twinkle in her eyes.

Frederick and Otto began helping Wee move in by carrying the heavier items.

Ayoka stood watching them in silence, with his arms folded and a look of disapproval on his face. He never offered to help. "Men do not do women's work. Paleface spoil their women. Come, Frederick, let's get a game of skinny started."

Wee smiled as she busied herself unloading the travois and setting up temporary housekeeping for her family. "Otto, go tend to the horses and rest for awhile. This is my people's custom. The women do the work. Men protect us from danger and do the hunting." Wee walked over and brushed his cheek lightly with her lips.

Otto took the hint. He had a feeling he was in the way.

Several of her Indian friends giggled. It was unusual for men to help them. And he was so handsome with that thick head of gray streaked black curly hair. Wee was one lucky woman, they whispered.

As Wee unpacked, she gave out several gifts, which she had purchased at the trading post before they came. She brought mirrors, combs, blankets, strouding for lodge covers, calico and denims, axes, needles, thread, kettles, frying pans, brushes, silk cloth, and jewelry for gifts to give her friends. She had to demonstrate the mirrors and other items to them. Dazzled by the gifts there was lots of pleasing "oohs and ahs" as the giggling women examined them gleefully.

CHAPTER 38

THE MEETING

Frederick and Ayoka rounded up several of the Indian youths for the strenuous game of skinny. The game was a popular game with the Indians. It was played with a leather ball the size of a grapefruit. You had to kick or hit the ball with a stick, but you could not touch it with your hands.

Several hours later, tired from playing the game, they sauntered over to Ayoka's grandfather's tent. The flap to Chief Big Horn's teepee was open, a sign of welcome. Before they entered, Chief Big Horn's teepee, Ayoka whispered in Frederick's ear, "Oh brother of mine, whatever happens inside, do not show any fear or anger." He continued, "Speak only when spoken to."

They walked in slowly, bearing to the right, Ayoka leading the way. Frederick noticed that the women walked to the left. Ayoka's grandfather was tall and straight. He had broad shoulders and well formed muscular limbs. His once handsome face had high cheekbones. You would never have known he was old, until you looked at his leathery and wrinkled skinned face. He had long thin white pigtails. Surrounding him in a circle were the elder councilmen of the tribe.

Frederick had a strange feeling that they had been expecting them. Chief Big Horn stood up pointing at two empty places on the floor next to him covered with buffalo skins. "Sit my sons." They sat down waiting obediently.

The Chief's voice was grave as he said, "I have known good Indian boys all of my life who have followed the rules of our tribe. Very few have disobeyed." He looked at Ayoka from under his bushy eyebrows. "My grandson, Ayoka is no different than other youths. He went to the sacred mountain, Pinnacle. Elders you must vote whether he is to be punished for disobeying."

The young man remained silent but looked downcast. He knew what his grandfather was talking about. All of his life, he had been told not to go to Pinnacle Mountain.

"Ayoka stand before the tribe, as they place judgement upon you. But first, do you have anything to say?"

Ayoka stood up. He turned, slowly gazing at each of the council members in the circle. Then he looked directly into his grandfather's eyes, saying, "I have disobeyed. I am ready to accept any punishment given me."

Frederick was proud of his blood brother. He admired his straight forwardness. He hoped the elders would feel this way. It was known throughout the plains that the toughest punishment given to anyone was running the gauntlet. An individual had to run between two lines of delirious Indians. They had to survive blows from clubs, tomahawks, axes, and knives. If they survived the test, they were heroes. Not many men came out alive, and if they did, they were maimed for life.

The councilmen gazed at Ayoka in a stoic manner, as if they were studying him. Ayoka remained standing. Each member got up and went over and huddled in the back of the lodge to deliberate the fate of Ayoka. Frederick silently made a wish as he crossed his fingers.

An hour passed. The silence was nerve-wracking to Frederick. Looking at Ayoka standing and not moving a muscle, he thought, only an Indian can be that patient. Finally one by one of the councilmen slowly walked back and sat down. The eldest man stood up before Chief Big Horn. "We have decided that Ayoka proved his pluck and courage by going to the mountain. We are proud of Ayoka. He has proved himself a man! This was his destiny. No punishment!" Everyone roared and clapped their approval.

The Chief nodded his head for them to return to their seat. He rose, as he said; "Now the medicine man will show his power."

CHAPTER 39

THE MEDICINE MAN'S POWER

In the middle of a circle, a fire surrounded by stones was blazing. A wiry little man sprinted out of nowhere. He was naked except for a breechcloth, moccasins, and a red sash wound his waist. There were two red-tipped hawk feathers in his hair and wide gold and silver bracelets on his forearms and ankles. Around his neck he wore a medicine bag. His face was streaked with red and white paint. In his hands were gourds. They rattled when he shook them. He leaped over to where Ayoka and Frederick were sitting, shaking the rattles in their faces. Their expressions remained impassive. A drum began to beat. He leaned over the fire and slowly washed his hands, face, and chest in the purifying smoke, and in a soft chanting voice said, "Great Spirit, give them the strength of a whole herd of buffalo. Show them where the Ta his ka (white buffalo) lives." He threw some black raven feathers into the fire. "Kong hee, (Raven), lead them to the sacred land of the Ta his ka." The smoke rose and swirled into fog-like circles. He hopped like a jackrabbit in front of both boys grabbing their hands. He pulled them into the circle of smoke. Handing each one of them a cup of liquid, he commanded. "Drink!" They drank. The medicine man screeched. Fire, smoke, sparks, and the beating of drums, TUM, Tum, Tum, TUM, tum, tum, pounded through the boy's temples. The intensity of the ritual, and the strange drink made them both swoon.

CHAPTER 40

A CURSE ON FREDERICK

When they came to, it was another day. The potion they drank had put them into a deep sleep all night. Chattering and giggling Indian women surrounded Ayoka and Frederick. Their bodies were being oiled with bear grease by massaging hands. The women rubbed their skin with soft deer cloth. Their skin gleamed. Both boys sat up at the same time. When they tried to stand up, they were gently pushed back.

One beautiful girl said, "Ayoka, you and your friend must be patient and not move. We are preparing you for another important meeting with Chief Big Horn. He will send for you soon. You must be ready!"

Ayoka nodded looking at Frederick. Frederick wiggled his dark eyebrows up and down. "Very pretty girl, Ayoka. We must do as she says." Then both of them held their sides as they laughed.

"Do not laugh at me!" the Indian girl said in an angry tone. Her cheeks flushed in anger.

Frederick could not help but admire her spunk. She possessed such an independent spirit. "Oh, oh." Frederick said, "If looks could kill, we would be dead."

"If you don't stop this talk at once, I will tell the medicine man to put a curse on you," she snapped.

Frederick said, "You are even prettier when you are angry. Tell me your name."

At this point Ayoka intervened. "Don't put a curse on him, Kysha. This is the one who saved my life. Frederick is my blood brother. We have fought side by side. We've shared danger and good fortune. We will risk anything for each other." Then clasping their hands together in a tight fist and raising their arms they yelled, "blood brothers Forever!"

"Oh, her name is Kysha. What a fitting name for one so beautiful." Frederick's eyes drank her beauty in with his bold dark eyes.

Ayoka tugged at her skirt. "Kysha has been saved for me. Someday she will be one of my wives."

Kysha put her nose in the air and walked over with the other women, who were peeking at them and whispering amongst themselves about the bravery and courage of the young braves.

Frederick looked surprised. "She will be a very lucky girl, Ayoka, to become one of your wives. And that custom of yours, of more than one wife, could cause a lot of trouble. If I had a jewel like her, I'd want her all to myself!"

Ayoka said, "You are kidding, aren't you? Does she appeal to my blood brother also?"

CHAPTER 41

THE DEADLY QUEST

One of the old Indian women sitting by the door walked over, saying, "It's time. Chief Big Horn is ready for you." She handed them each a bowl and pointed to her chewing mouth.

The flap to Chief Big Horn's tent was open. Ayoka and Frederick walked in. There was a large circle of men seated. One was Frederick's dad. Much to Frederick's surprise, the Indian, Bold One, who had delivered Ayoka's message of the coming celebration, was there too. When he saw them, his eyes showed no recognition. The peace pipe was being passed around and each man took two puffs from it.

Tall and dignified Chief Big Horn stood up and greeted his guests and friends. He held his hand up in a "Ho" sign. He was dressed in a soft buckskin robe, decorated with fringe and porcupine quill embroidery. His head was adorned with a full-length war bonnet on. His coup stick was trimmed with eagle feathers. The feathers showed his courage in hand-to-hand fighting. He motioned Ayoka and Frederick to sit by him. They sat. The pipe was passed to Ayoka. He took two puffs on it, passing it to Frederick. He lifted it to his lips, took one deep puff and started choking. Ayoka stifled a laugh and patted him on the back.

The 'At the Door Old Woman' brought a big iron pot of stew in and ladled some in each bowl. The savory smell drifted throughout the room. After tasting it, Frederick could not help but lick his lips. This was the best stew he had ever tasted. It was so good he finished his bowl and held out his bowl for more. This made the old woman very happy. Frederick watched his dad get a second helping too. He looked at Ayoka and said, "This is the best stew I have ever eaten." Taking his horned spoon, he fished up some of the large hunks of meat. Wee must get the recipe and make it at home."

Ayoka agreed, saying, "It's the gift of the gods."

After everyone ate, Chief Big Horn rose and taking an eagle feather from his headdress, he touched Ayoka with it. He spoke with great pride. "You have earned many coups (French for "blow") for your bravery, my grandson, Ayoka. I rename you 'Many Coups'.

Next he touched Frederick on the head, saying, "You saved my grandson, Ayoka, many times. Your Indian name is 'True Brave Friend'. You are not only a blood brother to Ayoka; you are a member of his tribe. Frederick glanced at his father, who smiled with pride.

Then Chief Big Horn called an Indian woman who was standing on the left side of the teepee. "Come here, Granddaughter." Wee walked slowly over to the Chief and handed him a package. The Chief opened it. Walking over to Ayoka he took an impressive bear tooth necklace out and placed it around Ayoka's neck. "Many Coups, here is your bear badge of courage and bravery necklace. You will receive great bear power from the bear's spirit.

Ayoka opened his mouth to speak, but a ferocious growl came out instead of his voice. The circle of men drew back in awe. This indeed was a mighty chief to be.

Chief Big Horn then walked over to Frederick placing the bear tooth necklace around his neck saying, "True Brave Friend, you also have bear power." Frederick kept his mouth closed, and just nodded.

The Chief turned back to Ayoka. He handed him a feather with a red spot on it. "This feather means that you killed your foe." Then he handed him another feather with notches on it. Each notch represented coups for bravery. "Many Coups, you must now complete your duty. Your vision was the mighty, sacred white buffalo. He is your protector and teacher. He will tell you what places are evil and his spirit will appear when you are in danger. You, Ayoka, have been given leadership qualities and a long life of plenty and adventure." Raising his lance above his head, he yelled, "You must hunt the white buffalo, your protector and kill him. After this meeting, choose your hunting party."

Then he took out a beautiful ceremonial pipe. In a solemn voice, he said, "This pipe is us. The stem is our backbone, the bowl our head. The stone is our blood, red as our skin." He passed the pipe around to each man who took a puff. When it returned to him, he began cleaning it. This was a sign for everyone to leave. The meeting was over.

THE MYSTERIOUS RECIPE

Ayoka made a quick silent departure. Frederick watched him ride with Chop Stix at a fast trot. He knew that Ayoka did not need company. He needed to be alone. Fredrick lingered behind talking to his father about the honors that had been bestowed on him and Ayoka.

Rubbing his stomach, he said, "I'm going to ask Wee to get that tasty stew recipe, before I forget it Pa."

"Do that son."

As Frederick entered the flap of their teepee, he commented to Wee on how nice everything looked. "Wee, while we were in the meeting, an old woman served us a delicious stew. Pa and I could not eat enough of it."

"Oh?" she said with a mysterious smile creeping across her face.

"Can you get the recipe, so you can make it for us at home?"

"I know the recipe Frederick. It's a dish my people serve at special occasions."

Frederick smiled. "How's it made?"

"Well you take a fat puppy, and put it in a large pot with herbs and different kinds of vegetables."

"You don't mean a dog, do you?" Frederick looked upset.

"That is our custom Frederick."

Without another word, Frederick rushed out of the teepee almost bumping into his father. He had to look for Wolf.

"Hey son, what's the hurry? Did you ask Wee to get the recipe for that great stew?"

CHAPTER 43

TOUGH DECISION

Ayoka and Chop Stix rode across the plains. He came to a barren slope. He picketed Chop Stix by a stream. He walked over to a giant moss covered rock and sat down. The pulse of the earth pounded in his temples. This was his quiet place to communicate with the spirits. He leaned forward from his seat, and stared intently toward the setting sun. He sat there for a long time in deep thought. He had to make a decision before the men of the camp began prodding him as to who was going to be chosen for the hunt. They would wheel and deal with him, pleading to be a part of the kill. He didn't want to kill his great protector, the mighty Ta kis ka, but if he shirked his duty, he would be thrown out of the lodge and be branded a coward throughout his life. Was there a solution? He knew that a man could never kill his protector, unless the protector gave himself to the hunter willingly. A full moon rose above the clouds along the horizon.

As he was praying the moon turned into his mentor's buffalo face, and in a deep voice broke the silence of the plains. "Brave means being fearful, but you must complete your Prophecy!" Then the silence of the earth prevailed.

Mounting Chop Stix, he raced back to the camp. Preparations had to be made soon for the deadly dangerous buffalo hunt. He would tell the crier to announce that the big buffalo hunt would be soon, and a council meeting would be held in the morning to plan and organize the hunt.

CHAPTER 44

THE PLANS

When morning came, the camp hummed with excitement. Fifty men were at the meeting, each one eager to be chosen for the hunt. Ayoka chose twenty men who were known for their brave deeds and fighting abilities. Ayoka explained, "There will be many more buffalo hunts. The ones I have not chosen will stay behind to protect the women, children, friends, and our old people."

Those men not chosen left the meeting. One of the men, Pony Boy stomped out with a bitter look on his face. He had not been chosen, because he was known as 'Bad Medicine'.

Pointing to Bold One, Ayoka said, "You, my childhood friend, faithful Bold One. You will be the marshal of the hunt. All of you chosen men are to obey his orders."

Bold One was proud, but humble. He and Ayoka had been best friends since they were babes in Cradleboard. He realized that nothing had changed between them. The trust and bond was still there. This appointment was a great honor and a step toward becoming a leader. Ayoka presented Bold One a scalp shirt and a feathered banner. This served as a symbol of his authority. Then Ayoka dipped his finger in black paint and drew a stripe down Bold One's right cheek. This was his badge of office.

Ayoka continued speaking. "The white buffalo will only be hunted by my blood brother and me. When you kill enough buffalo, Bold One will signal you to return to the camp. Frederick and I will not return until we find the Ta his ka. We will leave with your hunting party in the morning at daybreak." The chosen hunters stirred with anticipation. "Bold One, lay out your plans for the hunt, so the men can prepare themselves and their buffalo horses." Then he motioned for Frederick, and they left.

CHAPTER 45

THE ORDERS

Bold One stood straight and spoke. "We will only kill as many buffalo as the tribe needs for food and hides to last through the coming winter. No one is to go on the hunt until I give the signal. The hunt is dangerous, but it means food, clothing, and shelter for our people. He pointed at two of the braves, saying, "You are to keep order in the camp tonight. Make certain no one leaves to go hunting until morning."

During a hunt there were very strict rules. No one was allowed to go buffalo hunting by himself. Anyone who startled or stampeded the herd would be punished.

Pointing to two men, he said, "Swift Moccasin and Quick One, you are to scout for a buffalo herd. He then passed and cleaned the pipe. The meeting was ended.

When Bold One left the meeting, the women were congregating in-groups, waiting for him. He said, "Women have your dog or horse travois' ready in the morning to collect the dead buffalo and dress them out."

The chosen hunters left and checked on their best buffalo hunting horses. These horses were never used for workhorses. They were trained only for hunting, or racing. They patted them and praised them for their bravery in buffalo hunting. A hunter's life depended on the skill of his pony. If the hunted buffalo turned and charged, the pony had to know what to do. The hunter's aim had to hit the buffalo behind the shoulder blades. Their arrows or spears had to reach the heart. As they were readying their horses, they broke into song:

SIOUX WARRIORS SONG TO HORSE

My horse be swift in flight
Even like an eagle;
My horse be swift in flight.
Bear me now in safety
As we hunt the mighty buffalo.
And you shall be rewarded
With streamers and ribbons red.

S. BALDWIN

CHAPTER 46

ALL IS FAIR IN LOVE AND WAR?

That night the powwow celebration was in full swing with dancing, music and feasting. The Indians danced around by themselves to the throb of drums. The young men stood around watching and talking. Ayoka and Frederick eyed the different maidens who were standing in groups. Other girls sat in circles sharing secrets and laughing. The squaws (older women) stood in small groups, chatting and planning the day ahead, excited about the buffalo hunt. Others were tapping their feet to the drumbeat.

In the midst of the festivities, one of the men chosen to police the hunters came running up to Bold One. Breathlessly one of them said, "Pony Boy has sneaked out and is laying in wait for the buffalo."

Bold One was angry. Not only was the Indian in danger, he could ruin the hunt. This man had not been chosen for the hunt, because he never was good at obeying rules. He was 'Bad medicine'.

"Go, bring him back by force, if necessary." Bold One commanded. It was not long until Pony Boy was drug into the camp. A crowd surrounded him. His weapons were placed beside him, as he stood up, brushing dust from his clothes. In anger he spat at the women who were shaming and making fun of him. This was the worse punishment to be shamed in the eyes of the tribe. Then the women brought in some of his personal belongings. They took these belongings and threw them in the fire, shaming him as they did. His hunting arrows and bow were destroyed. Then the women chased him into his teepee, whipping him with willow branches. Before dawn he sneaked out like a shadow and was gone.

After that incident the dance continued as if nothing bad had occurred. The drums aroused Ayoka's emotions, and he sprinted out dancing to the beat of the tom-toms holding two rattles in his hands, shaking them vigorously. Kysha who was standing near tried to conceal a smile. She knew this was the beginning of the buffalo dance in honor of the hunt.

As he whirled around the floor a group of dancers wearing masks and buffalo horns and hides joined him. By imitating the animals, they hoped to be lucky to attract a herd to hunt. Ayoka danced around until he stood before Kysha. He removed his red sash lassoing it around her small waist, twirling her round and round. Her mother nodded in approval.

Coming back to where Frederick was standing, Ayoka took deep breaths saying with a glint in his eye, "Aren't you going to dance with one of the maidens, blood brother? Pick anyone you want."

Frederick didn't say a word, but his dark eyes met Kysha's. In slow steps he sauntered over to where Kysha was. Silently, he took her hand and pulled her on to the middle of the floor. The drums stopped beating. The buffalo men stopped their dancing and disappeared. Maidens placed their hands over their mouths in shock. Ayoka's woman to be was in the arms of another man. How daring! Placing his arm around her tiny waist, he drew her up to him. He bent down and whispered in her ear, "This is the way we palefaces dance. Just follow me. There was no music.

At first she tugged to get away, but he twirled her around and around without music. She began laughing.

"Daring Frederick, you want to get scalped don't you?" All of a sudden, she was jerked from his arms. Kysha fell to the floor. Her mother took hold of her long hair and drug her back with the women, giving Frederick a mean look.

A tomahawk whizzed by Frederick's ear with a vicious whistle and a menacing sound striking a tree, quivering back and forth. He walked over to a scowling Ayoka.

Frederick grinned a slow grin, saying; "All's fair in love and war. Right, blood brother?"

Ayoka's face was expressionless. Little did Frederick realize that when an Indian's dander is up that he had sooner die or make someone else die than to make a sound.

In a gruff voice, Ayoka said, "We have work to do."

Although the celebration was still on, Ayoka led Frederick towards the thicket to find Chop Stix and Gypsy. He pulled some feathers from his saddlebag. "Tie this necklace around Gypsy's neck. It will give her the power to run faster and easier." He opened a small bag filled with herbs. He handed a pinch of them to Frederick and said, "Do as I do, Frederick." He placed some of the herbs in Chop Stix' mouth and nostrils. Chop Stix sneezed. "This will give our horse's lots of needed strength in the hunt."

Frederick reached deep into his pocket. "Wee gave me this when she heard we were going on the hunt."

Ayoka looked at the blue cloth. There was one piece for him and one for Frederick. He knew it meant good luck. Ayoka attached it to his headband, and Frederick attached it to his hat.

As they readied their horses, Ayoka sang songs and prayers related to the medicine bundle of spirits.

A SIOUX SONG

We go to kill the white buffalo
The Great Spirit sent the vision
To look for him throughout the plains.
So give me my arrows; give me my bow;
I go to kill my Great Protector.

CHAPTER 47

CAMP IS RED WITH MEAT

At sunrise the camp hummed with excitement over the buffalo hunt. The chosen hunters were ready to go, dressed in their breechcloths and moccasins. Each hunter had twenty arrows strapped to his back. On his horse's neck was a long rawhide strap, which trailed behind the horse on the ground. This strap was to protect him. If he fell during the hunt, he could grab the trailing strap, slow the horse with his dragging body and pull himself to his feet. This way he could leap back on his horse.

When it was time for the hunt, the women took the teepees down. The long poles that were the foundation for the cloth teepees were now put to another use. They were used to make a travois, which trailed behind horses or dogs. The youth of the camp were involved too. They helped harness the horses and dogs that were pulling the travois' loaded with utensils to prepare the dead buffalo. Frederick noticed that all of the women had a heavy pack on their backs. He was amazed that the Indian women did such work, that paleface men did. They began moving slowly across the plains.

The chosen scouts rode far ahead of the marching people. Other braves acted as rearguards. This was an exciting time, and they sang The Buffalo Song as they marched along.

THE BUFFALO SONG

I go to kill the buffalo
The Great Spirit sent the buffalo
Over the plains and woods.

So give me my arrows; give me my bow;
I go to kill the buffalo

The dogs barked and the horses whinnied. The marshals picked the spot where they would pitch camp. The women put up the teepees and prepared the evening meal as the men gathered to chat and smoke. When they reached this area where they expected to hunt, the scouts fanned out across the countryside. Everyone waited in the quiet camp. Marshals moved quietly from one teepee to the next. They told the people in whispers not to sing or shout or make any loud noise that would scare off the buffalo. One of the scouts rushed back to camp telling Bold One that he had sighted the herd. Bold One charged up in the lead. Silently he led the other hunters forward and spaced them evenly, so that each would have a fair start. When they saw the buffalo, the men stayed downwind from the herd. This way the buffalo would not catch the scent of them. When they got close to the buffalo, they stopped and waited. Then crouching down like lizards over their horses the Indians sped toward the grazing herd.

The buffalo raised their heads sniffing the wind. Smelling danger, they stampeded down the prairie. The Indian braves raced after the fleeing herd with their strung bows, and spears. Most of the hunters had spotted the buffalo they intended to kill.

To carry only a spear on a hunt was a mark of daring and pride. Daring One was a brave who liked challenges and never took anything but a spear on a hunt. Yelling he charged after a ferocious looking bull. The bull was ready for him. With his long horns he gored Daring One's pony. Pawing the ground the crazed bull was going to finish him. Daring One leaped from the doomed pony, onto the buffalo herd and jumped lightly from one buffalo to another. Then taking his spear he plunged it into the heart of the maddened buffalo. Bold One saw this daring act and the immediate dilemma his friend was in. He galloped in the midst of the herd, and Daring One jumped on Bold One's horse. They sped out safely from the hunt. Jumping from their horses, they hugged one another, thumping each other on the back. Soon the hunt was over, and the hunters returned safely to the camp.

Now it was the women's turn to do their jobs. The women and maidens were all fired up about their camp being red with meat. They shouted thanks to Wonka Tonka and sang songs. Before the skinning and butchering started, a shaman chose one of the dead animals as a religious offering. One of the squaws removed the skin. This animal was to be a rare and sacred object. The rest of the carcass was left on the ground untouched where it had fallen. The spirit of the buffalo would find a resting-place there, and be pleased with the generosity of the hunters.

Each wife picked out the buffalo her warrior had killed. They recognized them by special markings on his arrows. The women in the hunter's household would be able to keep the hide. A huge campfire was built, and while the women worked, the men sat around the fire taking turns telling their stories and acting out the hunt. Bold One praised Daring One for his bravery and said he would be called, Many Buffalo Leaps.

The women and older girls worked diligently skinning and dressing the slaughtered animals. The women took sharp flint knives, slashed open the hides, and peeled them back. After a hide was removed, they butchered the meat. It was cut into pieces that could be bagged in buffalo skins and carried back to the camp. As the women worked on the meat, they took the men parts of the buffalo that spoiled quickly. The men ate warm liver on the spot. The women dragged the meat back to camp on their travois'. Bold One was proud of this hunt. As soon as they got back to camp, they had a big feast, sharing it with their guests.

The women were happy to get back to camp. Their work was cut out for them. They were kept very busy preserving the meat for the future. Meat was cut into strips and hung over high poles to dry. After several days, this sun-dried meat, called jerky, was so well preserved it would last for months. It could be carried anywhere and would not spoil, even during the hottest months.

The young women took the dried meat and pounded it to a pulp. They mixed it with buffalo fat, and flavored that with crushed nuts, berries, and fruit. This was called pemmican. Packed in buffalo-skin bags, pemmican would last for years without spoiling. Sliced and dipped in wild honey, it was nourishing and delicious, a favorite food among the Indians. The meat taken during a hunt was divided equally among all of the members of the band.

Extra meat and hides were set aside for the older ones, the sick, and for the orphans.

CHAPTER 48

KIDNAPPED

Kysha was tired and depressed. Although she had helped her mother and the other girls dress the buffalo from the hunt the hunters so successfully killed, the other girls completely ignored her. She knew they were jealous of the attention she had received from both Ayoka and Frederick. Her mother had whipped her with a hickory stick after they went to their teepee that night after the buffalo dance celebration.

Glancing towards the setting sun, she quietly slipped away down the path to the riverbank where a sparkling waterfall tumbled from high cliffs into a pool of water. She wouldn't be missed, because she went away by herself to this spot almost every day to fill the water jugs and take her bath. Her eyes held a dreamy look, different from their usual look of determination, as she began removing her deerskin dress slowly. She removed her beaded moccasins carefully and stepped into the cool water. Yawning and stretching her hands toward the shadowed mountains, she gave thanks to the Great Spirit for being alive. Closing her eyes and lifting her face upward, she felt the falling crystal clear water cleansing her body. But the soothing water would not erase the feelings she had. She had never felt this way before, not in all of her 15 years.

It had been planned that she and Ayoka would marry since they were little ones. Now she had doubts. Frederick with his brooding dark eyes looking at her the way he did and his strong muscular arms holding her tightly as he danced with her that special night. He was not a cowardly man. She remembered how her heart had pounded as if it wanted to be free. Free to marry anyone she herself would want. What could she do? Was she going mad? She was fascinated with Frederick. She had to be careful. White men fascinated several of the Indian maidens, and now she was following their pattern.

Ayoka was going to be Chief someday. All the other girls envied her, because she would be his woman. Ayoka was handsome, brave and kind. When he killed the white Ta his ka, the white fur would be made into a wedding dress for her. She would carry a purse studded with wampum. An especially fine robe would take ten days of steady labor for her mother to make. It was called a "silk robe" because of the softness of the leather and the sheen of the fur.

She said aloud, "I am so lucky. I will get that Frederick out of my head. What would I do if I married him? His woman would not do any work."

She hummed as she stepped out of the water on to the soft grass. Putting her dress back on, she sat down in the thick turf of greenery, laced with fern and mixed with lovely flowers. In a dream-like state, she brushed her long jet-black hair with long strokes with a brush made of buffalo bone. As she sat dreaming, she remembered how Ayoka always shared meat with her family. She helped her mother clean the hides from the animals he killed. Yes Ayoka was a good man.

After brushing her hair, she ran her porcupine-quill comb through her hair, so there would be no tangles. Then she plaited it. She reached into her dress pocket, taking out the beautiful red silk scarf Ayoka had given her, looping it around her neck.

Lying down she gazed at the deep azure never ending sky, mixed with wispy clouds. The music of the tumbling waterfalls relaxed her completely. She never noticed the tall swaying weeds having watchful eyes among them.

Soon the moon when the plums fall would be here and Frederick would go back to his way of life. That would be best, because down deep she knew that Ayoka would always be the brave for her. Dusk was falling, and stars were beginning to peek out of the sky. The moaning of the wind and the music of the tumbling waterfall sent her into a deep slumber. A shrill bird-like whistle pierced the air. She opened her eyes. It was very dark, and a hand covered her mouth. She fainted.

CHAPTER 49

THE LAND OF THE TA HIS KA (WHITE BUFFALO)

Ayoka and Frederick were disappointed that there wasn't any white buffalo in the herd. They had left the hunt early determined to find Ayoka's protector. They headed south over rough broken country, winding its way through deep canyons. They followed the river through wild and savage gorges and jagged cliffs, but now they were in easy rolling country with low hills.

Standing fast on a steep cliff overlooking the plains stood a regal white buffalo. He saw the two figures approaching. His eyes were sad. He knew they would come. It was time. He lowered his massive head and with his long bluish purple tongue licked on a crevice of salt. He had lived many moons. He was old and kept to himself, but he was still the leader of the Ta his kas. With a tremendous bellow, he made himself known. He turned and tramped slowly through the beautiful Gate of the Land of the White Buffalo.

Ayoka and Frederick had been riding for a long time. The sun had left the heavens. Twilight was settling in. It would be dark soon. Scanning the distant mountains, Ayoka and Frederick saw a speck a long way off in the distance. As they got closer it resembled a human. But when the bellowing rang out through the prairie, they saw a regal white buffalo standing high on a cliff. It had to be Ayoka's Protector. The horses picked their way warily as they ascended the steep incline of the mountain.

The path was jagged and full of juts. But when they got to the top of the cliff, the land changed dramatically. Darkness had engulfed them earlier. But now the clear shining sun rose over a vast land. A much-traveled path turned into a beautiful and easy trail. A trail made by buffalo. The terrain was white sand. The trees stood tall and were chalk white with barren limbs. An albino jack rabbit scampered across their path. A snow owl hooted in the barren branches of a tall tree. Ayoka looked back at Frederick. "Something is very strange. My heart feels a slight chill."

Frederick was rubbing his eyes. "Look at that tree over yonder. Look!"

Ayoka shaded his eyes looking in the direction Frederick was pointing.

"It's just a ghostly looking tree," he whispered.

"I swear Ayoka, the trunk was an Indian Brave with piercing eyes, dressed in white. He had curled horns on his head and a long tail. He was holding a sword."

Gypsy and Chop Stix twitched nervously. They could tell something was not right. Sensing danger, they continued at a slow gait along the pass.

Ayoka whispered. "You did see something Frederick. Look at that young tree trunk over there. It is an Indian maiden, possibly the White Buffalo Princess." They heard a rippling laugh sing out.

"When trees start looking like people and laughing, it's time for us to stop and rest. We are probably seeing mirages." Frederick said as he drew Gypsy to a halt and climbed down.

Dismounting Chop Stix, Ayoka stooped down putting his ear close to the ground. "I hear buffalo, and they are close by."

Frederick remained silent, pointing at the white sand with giant human footprint tracks, with a squiggly print of a snake like object trailing. A flock of white ravens swooped over their heads, calling, "Youuuuuu arrrr entering the Pte Ta Tryopa (Gate of the Buffalo)." Flying over their heads and flapping their wings, they flew ahead of them. Frederick cocked his gun. Ayoka kept his hand on his lance. As they followed the ravens, bushes filled with clusters of plump white grapes filled the air with their pungent fragrance. The boys eagerly popped them into their mouths.

Ayoka stooped down examining the prints in the sand. This is the land of thousands of buffalo. See the prints, Frederick?" Frederick stooped down looking at them. "This is the place where they winter. I can hear water singing." Staying in the brush, they parted the tall reeds. There stood hundreds of the Ta his kas. Some of them were contentedly lying in buffalo wallows. Ayoka was breathless; his eyes were ablaze with excitement. "We are in the magical virgin land of the Ta his kas. This is where the buffalo go when the chill comes over the land. The sun always shines here, and there is only daylight. Have you ever seen so many white buffalo and look at their thick hair? Let's make ourselves known."

When the buffalo saw them they did not stampede but kept chewing their cuds. Ayoka and Frederick slowly approached them, but the buffalo ignored them. "This is going to be an easy kill, Frederick, too easy." In the very front of the herd stood a magnificent bull, a little larger than the rest. He was staring at them.

"There he stands, the great protector, Ayoka. Kill him before he gets away!"

Ayoka raised his bow drawing his arrow back.

The bull took a few steps closer to him, as if to say, "Here I am, your protector. Kill me and wear me well."

In a forcible manner Ayoka slung his bow to the ground. "Look at him! I can't do it Frederick. He is sacrificing himself to me! I will let my tribe banish me. If this is what it takes to be Chief, then I do not want it!" Frederick knew that his blood brother was dead serious.

When he yelled and threw this tantrum, the white buffalo herd looked up. They panicked and stampeded across the river. But the white bull just stood there.

"Let's get out of here, Frederick. I am not going to kill him!" He turned to look at his blood brother. Where was he? Where the white bull stood was a gigantic half man and half buffalo. There were curled buffalo horns on his head, and he had masses of bushy white hair. His partly closed eyes were weak, and he blinked in the sunlight. He had a long tail sweeping the ground. In one hand he held an enormous shield, and in the other hand was a long sword. He began circling an object. It was Frederick. He was lying on the ground as if he were dead. Ayoka stooped down placing his hand on Frederick's heart. He could not feel a heartbeat. Hovering white vultures were perched on the barren tree limbs ready to swoop down and savor his body.

The Buffalo Man raised his sword above his head swishing it through the air. In a thundering voice that shook the earth, he said, "You and your friend are about to be killed!" He moved towards Ayoka with his sword drawn. The rays of the sun shot flashes of blinding glares from its sharp blade.

Ayoka stood up completely fearless. Without a thought in his head but to save his blood brother, he let out a "Whoop" drawing his lance from its sheath. At full running speed, he charged towards the Buffalo Man with his lance held high. The Buffalo Man guarded himself well with his shield. Ayoka leaped into the air swinging his lance. It struck the shield and busted. He quickly dove to the ground, grabbing pieces of the shattered lance. As the giant came towards him, Ayoka held the gleaming lance piece towards the sun throwing blinding flashes of light into the buffalo man's weak eyes. The Buffalo Man rubbed his eyes and stumbled all around. Blinded he dropped his shield and lance. Ayoka got to his feet and shot three arrows in quick succession, all of them zinging straight into the Buffalo Man's unprotected heart. He slowly crumpled to the ground.

"I, Ayoka, Many Coups have killed him!" His voice rang throughout the mountains and valleys. Ayoka ran over to touch him with his coup stick, but it was not the Buffalo Man he was touching. It was the white buffalo bull, his Protector.

Ayoka fell to his knees, kneeling over him, placing his hand under his head. His Protector was breathing laboriously and frothing heavily. Blood was gushing out of his heart.

Ayoka cried, "You tricked me into killing you, my great Protector." Ayoka placed his arm under the buffalo's head, cradling him and chanting softly.

The white buffalo sighed, saying in a low whisper, "You have earned the four virtues of a great Chief, Ayoka; Generosity, Bravery, Wisdom, and Fortitude. Prophesy Fulfilled. Wear me well great Chief!" Then he closed his eyes and let out a deep audible breath and died.

Tears streamed down Ayoka's face. Then he heard sighs, like the Chinook wind. Looking up, he saw the buffalo herd standing near. He went to take his arm out from under his Protector, but all he held was a thick beautiful white hide, no bones and no blood. His Protector had left an unblemished wedding robe for his wife to be Kysha.

Looking up and blinking his eyes, he could not believe what he was seeing. Rubbing them he jumped to his feet. There stood the Buffalo Man. Ayoka was shaken and awed by the sight of him. He was dead! He had killed him! He tried to turn and run for cover, but he couldn't move. His body was frozen. He tried to speak. His lips were sealed. He was unable to work any of his body parts.

The Buffalo Man picked up the buffalo skin. He walked over to Ayoka and placed it around his shoulders. He said in a familiar voice Ayoka had heard before, "Go to your people. You shall become the youngest and greatest Chief of the Sioux Indians. But in order to release me you must take your coup stick and tap me with it." He bowed, knelt and bowed his head.

Ayoka, trembling, raised his hand with the coup stick. He was able to move. He gently tapped the Buffalo Man with it. A huge white cloud forming a thick misty fog slowly descended and engulfed the Buffalo Man, forming a path upward towards the heavens. The magnificent Buffalo Man led his herd at a methodical pace up the path towards the heavens. They were going to the Happy Hunting Ground.

Ayoka knew in his heart that he would see his Protector again someday. He bowed his head in prayer giving thanks to Wakan Tanka (Sioux God). Then he ran over to look for Frederick. He was lying on the ground groaning. Checking him out, he was relieved to see there was no blood. Frederick sat up. He looked confused.

"Frederick, you okay?"

"Why in the tarnation shouldn't I be brother?"

"Blood brother, lots has happened." Then he began telling him everything that had occurred.

Frederick gazed into Ayoka's dark watered up eyes. Looking at Ayoka with the magnificent white buffalo robe around his shoulders, he said. "You did it Ayoka. You fulfilled your prophecy." Clasping their hands together in a tight fist and raising their arms, they yelled, "blood brothers Forever!"

Gypsy and Chop Stix came trotting up. They mounted them and raced full speed ahead towards the camp.

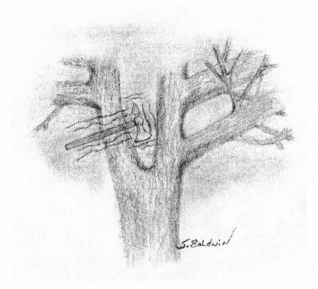

S. Baldwin

CHAPTER 50

SMOKE MEANS TROUBLE

As they rode close to the Black Hills, Ayoka pointed to three puffs of smoke at a time rising in the distance. The Great Council Fire was burning. It was a signal for help. Ayoka said, "Something is wrong at our camp." He urged Chop Stix into full speed. Frederick and Gypsy followed.

In the distance they saw a cloud of dust. Soon they spotted a rider riding hard across the plains. It was Bold One. Ayoka yelled "Ho!" Ayoka drove his heels into Chop Stix's sides, racing to meet him.

Bold One skidded to a halt, jumping off his horse. His face was laced with anger. He hurled his hatchet into the ground. This meant death and defiance. Ayoka and Frederick jumped off of their horses. Ayoka spoke, "Speak brother. What has happened?"

Bold One struggled for his breath and finally choked out, "The Cheyenne raided our camp last night, taking our prize ponies and horses."

Ayoka surprised Frederick and Bold One by roaring with laughter. "So, we'll go on a revenge raid to their camp, and bring back some of their prized horses with ours."

Bold One did not laugh. His face was iron clad, and his manner was sullen. His black eyes narrowed forming slits above his high-cheeked masklike expression. Clenching his teeth together, he said "Don't make light of this Ayoka. They have taken Kysha."

Leaping on Chop Stix, Ayoka let out a war-hoop. "They have the blood of cowards. We shall kill them like dogs."

In this sudden and gloomy change of attitude, Frederick whipped Gypsy to a full gallop following Ayoka towards the Black Hills. They had to do something quick. Kysha's life was in danger, if not taken already. All three of them galloped at top speed until they reached the camp. The women and braves ran to meet them. The camp was in complete chaos. Kysha's mother was crying. Her wrinkled face looked older than he remembered it. "Ayoka, please save our Kysha. The Cheyenne's have kidnapped her."

Ayoka climbed down from Chop Stix. He removed his white buffalo robe and handed it to Kysha's mother. "Never fear, I shall save Kysha, Mother. Meanwhile pray to the Wakan Tanka that we have success in getting our horses back. Keep yourself busy by working on a beautiful wedding robe for your daughter. I intend to take her for my wife soon."

This consoled her and she turned going back to her teepee to pray and begin making the dress. She and her husband had a lot of faith in Wakan Tanka and Ayoka.

Frederick looked around for his dad and Wee. They had left for home. Tension and suspense filled the air. Ayoka looked at Frederick saying. "Frederick, this isn't your fight. Go home. We shall meet again."

Frederick looked at his blood brother in a crushed and disheartened way. There was coolness in Ayoka that he had not seen before. This was something he had not expected. How could he dismiss him this way? After all they had been through together. But again his dauntless spirit rose. "I'm not a quitter

Ayoka. Your fight is my fight!" Clasping their hands together and raising their arms high into the air, they yelled "blood brothers Forever!"

Bold One stood watching them. Pointing to himself, he said, "Me go too. Ayoka's fight, my fight also!"

Ayoka grabbed him and hugged him. "Thank you, true friend of mine!"

A council meeting was quickly held. Ayoka chose the nine best trackers in the camp who figured out the rescue plan. Even though the enemy had slipped away, the trackers knew they were the crafty Cheyenne's. They had taken the best horses of Chief Big Horn and other braves. Bold One said, with an angry look, "Spy among us. Raiders know too much about our camp."

Ayoka was overcome with grief. He shook his head, saying, "When we catch the culprit, he will run the gauntlet, and will be put out on the plains for the buzzards to feast upon."

The men planned an early dawn journey by foot. "We must leave before the sun rises," Bold One said..

Early morning came and the men were prepared to leave. As they crossed the river, Frederick saw strands of long black hair with a piece of red silk waving in the breeze on a branch. He pointed it out to Ayoka.

Ayoka growled, "I gave her that scarf. If they harm a hair on her head, I will choke them with that scarf."

They hiked through the brush and tangled wilderness being careful not to break a branch or twig. The least suspicious sound would alert Kysha's captors, and they would immediately tomahawk her. Soon they came to where a fire had been made. The ashes were still luke-warm. The traces grew fresher by the moment. They were hoping they could catch the enemy before they reached their tribal village. Soon they came to a high bluff. Crawling on their bellies like snakes, Ayoka and Frederick saw hundreds of teepees below.

CHAPTER 51

THE GET-A-WAY

It was nightfall at the Cheyenne camp. The night was silent except for the howling of the wind and the whining of the horses below. There was lots of activity and celebration going on. The pounding of the drums and "War-hoops" echoing through the air meant the teepees would be empty.

Ayoka instinctively scanned the dark blur of the woods with an anxious eye making sure no enemies were present. He then sent five of the trackers down to spy and find out the whereabouts of Kysha. Stealing the horses back from them would be no trouble, but getting Kysha back would depend on the luck of the gods and his mighty Protector. Meanwhile the rest of them would try to get a little shut-eye. The moon with the face of a buffalo beamed brightly.

Bold One said, "You shut eye. I keep lookout." He shimmied up one of the cottonwood trees onto a sturdy limb overlooking the camp. Bold One had brought a long rope. He tied it around the limb. He had a purpose and did not foresee any flaws in his plan.

Frederick lay all night with his back against the tree with his rifle across his lap. It was the same tree that Bold One was in. After awhile he dozed off. Ayoka, knife in hand dozed off too. This was what Bold One was waiting for. Taking hold of the rope he swung out from where the rest were sleeping, landing a safe distance away. His moccasin feet skimmed the earth like a light-footed deer, and it wasn't long before he was on the outskirts of the enemy camp.

CHAPTER 52

THE BOUNTY

The Cheyenne raiders galloped in the camp at full speed bringing the horses they had gotten from the Sioux camp. Indian squaws, maidens, young and old braves greeted them with shrieks and screams of joy at the magnificent horses they had stolen. But then a hush came over the gathering. One Indian warrior had a beautiful Indian maiden on his horse with waist length dark wavy hair, and a red torn silk scarf around her neck. An old woman ran up and jerked the scarf from Kysha's neck. Kysha reached down and slapped her, leaving a handprint on her face. Then she jerked her scarf back. An indignant squaw yanked her down from the horse. Another one grabbed her by her long shining hair and drug her to the center of the circle where a fire blazed. Kysha clamped her teeth into the woman's arm and wouldn't let go. The Indian woman let out a scream releasing her quickly. Kysha stood up brushing the dirt from her dress. She was breathing hard.

The warrior who had kidnapped her, dressed in full war regalia, dismounted his horse. He circled her measuring every inch of her with his hungry eyes. Then in an authoritative voice, he said, "Speak. Who are you?"

Her blood raced, but she confidently tossed her head. "I am Kysha who will be the wife of Ayoka soon to be Chief of the Sioux Tribe in the Black Hills. She pointed her finger at him, "You kidnapped me. Who are you?"

"I am the Chief's adopted son of this Cheyenne camp. Looking at her from under bushy black eyebrows, he said. "I have heard of this Ayoka. He has the reputation of being very brave and has earned many coups. But me know better. He is nothing but mixed up chicken livers. No doubt he will be after you, if I let you live."

"Yes he will! Her dark eyes snapped. And he will spit on your grave, if any harm comes to me." She stomped her foot on the ground. She felt evil all around.

Smirking he said. "Ayoka's little wife to be has lots of spunk." He raised his hand and motioned to a medicine man. "Take her to my lodge and guard her well until I make my decision as to her future."

The scary looking medicine man in his breechcloth grabbed her arm. She jerked away from him. "And what decision will that be?" She placed her hands on her hips.

"Well my saucy one, the gods might shine down on you to become one of my wives if you cooperate.

"Never!" she screamed.

In a cruel edge to his voice, he said, "And if you don't, I will sell you to one of those palefaces." She knew not to let the tears fall, but she could not help it. That was a sign of weakness. As a tear rolled down her face, he put his face in hers, leering at her cruelly and continued. "Or I will burn you at the stake or make you a sacrifice to the gods. Then he roared saying, "Get her out of my sight."

Kysha was trying to put on a brave front, but she was full of fear. She glanced up at the full moon. Was the moon the face of a buffalo? She quickly looked back at him. The brightness of the night threw more light on his face. She peered at him suspiciously. There was something familiar looking about him or was it his voice? The Wakan Tanka is angry with me, because of my thoughts concerning Frederick. She trembled. The medicine man grabbed her arm and drug her to a large teepee. He threw her on a bear rug on the teepee floor and bound her wrists together. Her whole body was aching and sore. It was hard for her to move. She lay there in deep thought. What was she going to do? What was in store for her? A guard stood at the entrance. Ayoka would come after her. She knew it. And Frederick would be with him. She heard voices coming from the back of the teepee and the snapping of twigs and leaves rustling. Then an owl in the distance hooted. She didn't know that this was a signal to Bold One's friends, letting them know he was in enemy camp. After the Cheyenne Indians quieted down and went to their teepees, the firewater they had drunk drugged them, sending them into a deep slumber. If they did wake up, they would be so intoxicated; they would not be able to defend themselves.

CHAPTER 53

KYSHA IS ALIVE!

Bold One and the trackers met just outside the camp. They told Bold One that they had seen Kysha being drug into the teepee and was guarded well by a medicine man. Bold One told the trackers in a quiet voice to steal their horses back and take some of their horses and head back to where Ayoka and Frederick were while the camp was in this dead sleep. "I will stay. Tell Ayoka when they hear an owl hoot four times, it is a signal that Kysha and I are safe, and for them to hightail it back to the Sioux camp."

The trackers, running on fleet feet, moved carefully to the silent camp cutting the best horses loose that had been tethered. They headed back up the mountain at a quickened pace.

Bold One crept to the back of the teepee where Kysha was imprisoned. Lying on the ground, he covered himself with leaves, making noise on purpose. The medicine man guard heard this and crept around to the back of the tent with his raised tomahawk in hand. When he stepped on the leaves, Bold One grabbed his leg. He pulled him down and tomahawked him. Then he scalped him. He quickly put the medicine's man's clothing on and the ugly mask. Holding the medicine man's spear, he stood straight as an arrow at the teepee opening guarding the door. He heard someone coming.

It was one of the Cheyenne braves. He brushed by Bold One nearly knocking him down. Bold One recognized the Indian as Pony Boy. So that was the spy. But what was he doing here in the Cheyenne camp? He listened.

"Wake up my pretty one! I have made my decision. I know what I am going to do with you!"

Kysha opened her eyes. She had not been asleep. She looked up at the savage. His paint had been washed off of his face. She had seen him before. Now she remembered. "Pony Boy, it's you! What are you doing here? You knew who I was all along!"

"I am the Chief's adopted son. Me important here. I will get many coups for raiding your camp and stealing you." He reached down and untied her wrists, jerking her to her feet, facing him. "You will marry me," he said, as he fingered her long hair. The old Chief will not live much longer. Then I will be Chief of this tribe soon. We will have many little papooses together."

She cringed, "No! I am going to marry Ayoka. You are a traitor, a disgrace to your own people!" Her voice portrayed disgust.

He grabbed her long hair, pulling her head back putting a knife to her delicate throat and tickling it with the pointed sharp blade. He stared into her eyes with unquenchable hatred. "You ain't in no position to tell me what to do. You're on my turf now. Since you won't cooperate you shall be given as a sacrifice to me. I shall get revenge from Bold One and Ayoka."

"Demon!" she screamed.

CHAPTER 54

TO THE RESCUE

Just then the medicine man leapt in. Pony Boy had an astonished look on his face, when the man he thought was of his tribe was coming toward him with a menacing look. Drawing his knife away from her throat, but still holding her by the hair, he cried, "What's wrong with you Shaman (medicine man)? Have you had a little too much firewater? It is me, Pony Boy!"

The medicine man struck him with a mighty blow. Pony Boy lost his grip on Kysha. She scrambled to the back wall. The two men began to grapple, hand to hand fighting. They fell to the ground rolling over and over. Kysha saw a huge vase nearby. This was her chance to save Bold One. Grabbing it she ran up to the fighting men and smashed it over one of their heads.

"Thanks Kysha." It was Pony Boy talking. She had hit the wrong man. He pulled his knife out and grabbing Bold One's hair raised the dagger into the air. Kysha hid her eyes.

Then a mighty yell pierced the air as a tall Indian, with strong bronze muscular arms rippling grabbed Pony Boy's wrist, and with a force of superior strength broke his hold on the knife just in time. A hoarse voice between a whisper and moan only audible to Pony Boy said, "You've just signed your death decree, Pony Boy." The knife spun across the floor. Locked in vicious hand to hand blows Ayoka and Pony Boy fought a fierce battle. Pony Boy retrieved his knife. He raised his hand with the knife poised at Ayoka. Struggling with all of his strength to wrench the knife from Pony Boy's hand he twisted Pony Boy's wrist around with the knife pointing at his heart. Pony Boy stabbed himself in the chest and was killed instantly. After Ayoka lifted his scalp, he screamed, "Die Traitor Dog! You're on your way to Netherland!"

Hearing Ayoka's voice Kysha ran to him, throwing her arms around him. "Oh Ayoka, you are so brave, but I mistakenly hit Bold One with the vase."

Ayoka took advantage of the moment and held her tightly in his arms. "Don't worry my woman. All is well!" She stood there with her head resting on his shoulder.

Bold One sat up rubbing his head. He jumped to his feet saying, "Me Ok. You give good wallop Kysha." All of them laughed. By this time the commotion had aroused the enemy Indians.

The whooping began and several of Indians stormed the lodge. Seeing the chief's adopted son lying stabbed to death on the ground aroused their anger.

Ayoka yelled to Bold One. "Run Bold One and take Kysha to safety. I will hold them off." As Kysha was being drug off by Bold One, she screamed, "Ayoka, let me stay with you." Slitting an opening in the back wall of the tee-pee, Bold One pulled unwilling and strong willed Kysha through to the back where a horse was waiting.

CHAPTER 55

WHEN THE SUN IS STRAIGHT ABOVE THE TREES

Ayoka didn't have a chance. Several of the Cheyenne Indians grabbed him. They dragged him out to the center of the camp, tying him to a pole. Morning was just dawning. The women began taunting him and throwing dirt and stones in his face. Ayoka did not grimace. All he could think of was, "It's my time to die. But where is Frederick?" The sun threw its hot rays down on him drenching him with sweat. He began the death song.

The men went into the Chief's tent informing him of the intruder. The Chief immediately called a council meeting. "Go get this intruder. Bring him to me! We will let him talk before we decide on his punishment."

Two men, treating Ayoka with scorn, drug him in. His face was caked with mud and blood. As he stood straight as an arrow, although his body was bruised and aching, before the Chief, a woman brought water and a damp cloth wiping his face with it. She had a compassionate look on her face. Then she stroked his hair with her hand. She was the Chief's daughter, Big Blossom, the widow of Pony Boy. Her body was covered with marks of abuse.

The Chief couldn't help but notice a regal bearing about this young brave. "Speak Intruder. Who are you? What brought you here killing my adopted son?"

With eye contact, Ayoka stared at the elderly chief. Words began tumbling from his mouth. "My name is Ayoka, the grandson of Chief Big Horn of the Sioux Tribe. The man you call your adopted son was of our Sioux tribe. He deserted us. He would not follow our laws or rules. He ran away. He was gone for many moons. One night he came back to our camp. He led the raid with some of your men capturing our best horses. That wasn't enough, he stole my wife to be who was sleeping by the riverbank waiting my return, and was forcing her to marry him or he was going to have her sacrificed to him. A hush fell over the complete lodge, with the Chief staring intently at Ayoka.

"Continue Ayoka."

"My loyal friend was outside the tent when he heard Pony Boy threaten my woman with a knife. He charged in as Pony Boy put the knife to her throat. Seeing my friend, he slung my woman to the floor and was aiming the knife at my friend's throat. That's when I ran in and grabbed his hand to save my friend. My intentions were to get the knife from him, but by a twist of fate, he turned it towards his own body and plunged it deep into his heart. I told my friend to take my woman back to our camp. The noise aroused your people."

The chief said, "I know your Grandfather, Chief Big Horn well. I know that a grandson of his would not lie. I do not blame you for raiding back your own horses. That is an honor among our tribes. But my adopted son being killed over a woman cannot be excused. Why didn't you do the honorable thing and come directly to me?"

"I didn't know if the Cheyenne Tribe had a good, fair Chief. Time wasn't on my side. I couldn't take chances, and I didn't want the woman I planned to marry dead." There was a murmur among the tribe people.

"You are young, Ayoka, and I have heard from many voices about your bravery, but you will have to be punished." He pointed to the woman standing on the left side of the tent. "Pony Boy was married to my daughter, Big Blossom. Now she is without a husband. By rights she is entitled to your scalp or I can give you to her, and she may torture you as she pleases! Elders go communicate with the spirits and see what his punishment will be. Death or leniency."

Looking at the older woman with unkempt hair, Ayoka thought I would rather be dead, than be given to his daughter. The elders went to the corner of the lodge. They whispered. In a short time the leader walked before the Chief. "Chief Many Horses, we have come to a decision." Ayoka turned to learn his fate. He did not have a good feeling.

Chief Many Horses said, "Speak!"

The oldest man spoke. "To teach him patience, he must run the gauntlet. If he succeeds and reaches the end of the line still standing up, he shall be honored and exalted. If not we shall scalp him alive, and let the vultures feast upon his body."

Chief Many Horses said, "So be it!" Looking at Ayoka sternly, he said, "If you are still living, I shall give my daughter, Big Blossom, to you as one of your wives. She is entitled to this."

Ayoka looked over at the Chief's daughter who was smiling and nodding her head up and down, meaning that this decision would please her. He suddenly felt ill. The Chief said. "Ayoka, since I am a friend of your Grandfathers, I am going to let you roam about our camp until tomorrow as a free man. You can go about our camp of your own free will but without any protection. Your weapons will be taken and destroyed. If you try to escape, we will hunt you endlessly and shoot your body full of arrows. When the sun is straight above the trees, your punishment will begin. Do you have anything to say?"

Ayoka was thinking. He stared into space. To run the gauntlet was to run between two lines of frenzied savages and receive blows from their clubs, tomahawks axes, and knives. He doubted he would ever leave the camp alive. If he made the 'running of the gauntlet' he would be mutilated for life. He would be shunned for life because of his ugliness. Kysha would want someone else. But there was one thought in Ayoka's mind. He had to communicate with his mentor and the spirits, but in a sacred place. "Chief, I would be better off dead than the punishment given me, but I will do my best to survive."

In a patient voice the chief said, "Son do you have any wishes before the sun is straight above the trees tomorrow?"

"Yes, I would like to go into the hills and communicate with the spirits. I will not try to escape, but I would like you to provide me with a buffalo skull and a pipe.

"Wish is granted," the Chief said. He motioned to his daughter. She waddled over to him holding her blanket snuggly around her, grinning shyly.

In a kindly gesture, the chief handed Ayoka two buffalo rocks for luck. "We will send smoke signals to your tribe, asking them to come. Go! You are a free man until tomorrow."

CHAPTER 56

A MYSTERIOUS FRIEND

Ayoka knew he would be well guarded, and if he did try to escape, he would be killed on the spot. But he was still wondering, "Where in the tarnation is my blood brother?" He fingered his medicine bundle. He found his way through the adjoining forest until he came to a small brook with a grassy knoll. He stooped down and made a small fire, and took charcoal and sweetgrass smearing his body. Then he sat down and placed the buffalo skull at his feet. He pointed the pipe towards the sky and began rocking back and forth chanting. He sang and prayed asking for supernatural powers in running the gauntlet. Big Blossom was peeking at him from the bushes.

It was a mystic night, as black as coal. Then as Ayoka prayed, the howling of a wolf broke the silence. The howling was getting closer and closer. Ayoka took a stick and stirred the dying embers of the fire. Looking into the brush he saw piercing eyes glowing and the howling grew more intense. Ayoka was without weapons. He was a doomed man. Closing his eyes, rocking back and forth, and praying to his mentor and the Great Spirit he soon fell asleep.

While he had his eyes closed a thick white fog blanketed the earth, depleting the darkness. It was so thick it covered him and everything around him. Ayoka grew warm and comforting. The only obstacle showing was the smiling face of the Buffalo moon.

Ayoka woke with a start to something cold touching his nose. He opened his eyes. He was staring into a pair of electrified eyes. It was a huge white wolf, the largest wolf he had ever seen in these parts. The wolf was baring his teeth as if Ayoka was a morsel of food.

Ayoka was on his feet with one bound. Big Blossom crashed out of the brush and handed a tree limb to him. Ayoka grabbed it and whacked the wolf on the nose. The wolf snatched the limb from Ayoka's hand, and showing his teeth, looked at him with a grotesque grin. Ayoka was stunned at the bravery of this woman. To think she wanted to save him, and put her life in danger!

The wolf turned growling and grabbed hold of Big Blossom's skirt, ripping it off of her, showing black bloomers. She tore off running towards the camp frantically screaming with the wolf close behind her.

Ayoka suddenly felt like laughing. He didn't know why with the dangerous predicament he was in. But he exploded with laughter.

The wolf came back and lay down at Ayoka's feet. Something is strange about this creature, Ayoka thought. He acts almost human. Could he be a werewolf?

The morning sun came up brightly, throwing shadows through the trees. The dew was heavy on the ground. Instead of feeling exhausted, Ayoka was full of new energy. His body felt electrified and renewed. Exuberance possessed him. He felt full of strength and power. And he was famished. He took off running like an eagle towards the camp where the women were cooking breakfast. The wolf followed running on his hind feet behind him. The women watched Ayoka and shook in their moccasins when they saw a wolf running like a human. One old woman had just filled a bowl with grits and cornbread. Ayoka, with the mannerisms of an animal snatched the bowl from her, shoving the food in his mouth. Then he handed the bowl to her pointing to it and then to his mouth meaning more. In a demanding voice, he yelled, "Me hungry! More!" The white wolf came up behind Ayoka and howled loudly.

The women became frightened and left running wildly in all directions, dropping their cooking utensils and running into their teepees. Ayoka and the wolf ate all the food.

Big Blossom had run into the Chief's tent. She said, "What kind of Indian brave is this who is going to be killed at noon and is ravishingly eating all of the food? Why he should be frightened out of his breechcloth. Not only that, but a fierce wolf ripped my clothing." She fanned herself with her hand.

One Indian brave ran out with a strung bow and let the arrow go "Zing" straight towards the wolf's heart. The wolf was still standing up on his two hind legs like a human. He caught the arrow with his sharp fanged teeth and took it over to Ayoka. The Indian brave who shot the arrow turned, and like a streak of lightning shot into the Chief's lodge. Ayoka stared at the wolf in amazement. He tossed the wolf a large chunk of buffalo meat.

With all of this commotion, Chief Many Horses went to the door of his lodge and looked out at Ayoka and the wolf. He shook his head back and forth in silence. It was a shame for such an Indian brave to die, especially since he was the grandson of his friend Chief Big Horn.

THE GAUNTLET

It was minutes before high noon and men and women began lining up forming two lines for the gauntlet, armed with all kinds of weapons. At the start of
the two lines stood two tall bald headed muscle-bound men swinging their
clubs with balled spikes on their ends in the air. They were bloodthirsty and
ready to smash Ayoka's brains out. The excited crowd was yelling insults at
Ayoka. All except one Indian woman, Big Blossom. She hovered over by Chief
Many Horse's teepee covering her eyes.

Ayoka raced over to the start of the gauntlet lines. He was eager to begin the
challenge. The white wolf followed closely at his heels with a snarled lip and
raised hackles.

Entering the circle of the teepees on his handsome Palomino horse, Sabine,
decorated with plumes and paint was his Grandfather, Chief Big Horn, in full
war regalia. His impressive warbonnet full of eagle feathers represented all of
his coups and hung to the ground. His highbred horse danced under him.

Following him was Ayoka's perky little mule. Chop Stix brayed and pranced
when he saw his master. He knew that his master was going to be killed today
and he would be killed also, so he could join his master at the 'Happy Hunting
Grounds'. Chief Big Horn promised him he would be killed painlessly, and he
would be buried with honors. Chop Stix turned and trotted bravely up to his
master for one last nuzzle. Then arching his neck, he turned and trotted back
to Chief Big Horn.

Ayoka turned and waved his hand at his Grandfather saying, "Grandfather,
it's a good day to die."

Chief Big Horn raised his hand in a farewell sign.

Chief Many Horses held his hand high in the air with a thunderstick in his hand. "When I fire the thunderstick, run like the wind Ayoka. May the gods be with you!"

CHAPTER 58

THE CONQUEST

"Baam!" went the thunder stick. A bright flashing thunderbolt of lightning zig-zagged through the sky and crashed down to where Ayoka stood. A thunderous clap of thunder deafened all ears and the ground shook. Although the day had been bright, blackness enveloped the whole area. The horses whinnied. Screams and chaos filled the air. People stumbled into each other running for cover. One yelled, "It is the Thunder Bird. He is angry."

Chief Many Horses called out. "My tribe! Do not run! Hold your ground." He called to Ayoka. "Where are you?" He'd seen the flashing thunderbolt strike where Ayoka was standing, and he thought it had struck Ayoka dead.

Chief Many Horse's voice called out again to his people. "Do not run. Hold your ground. Stay where you are! Ayoka may be dead."

A tremendous roar deafened their ears again. The ground trembled. The sun broke through with shining rays thwarting out the blackness. The tribal people forming the gauntlet crouched down on the ground. When daylight appeared again they jumped to their feet holding their weapons high. But when they looked at where Ayoka had been standing, they shrunk back and gasped in horror.

Ayoka was standing like a stone and white hair was growing and covering his whole body. White fangs protruded from his mouth, and saliva was dripping from it. Ayoka was no more. In his place stood a huge albino maddened bear! Standing on his hind legs, his huge head wagged side to side glaring at them with fire shooting out of his eyes. His once human hands were long claws slashing through the air.

The giant warriors swung their clubs to bash the bear's brains out! They were no match for the enormous bear, but though they were trembling with raw fear, they stood their ground. If they ran like cowards, they would be killed. The bear lumbered down the path snatching the clubs from the shirking participants and busting them to pieces. The long line of Indians scampered in all directions like a bunch of scared rabbits.

Chief Big Horn had stood his ground with Chop Stix all this time. He called out; "Ayoka has bear power, earned by his mighty brave feats. Your tribe is no match for him. You must free him."

The bear continued down the gauntlet path until he reached the end. When he stopped, he turned around, and roared loudly, beating his chest in victory.

The white wolf standing on his hind feet howled one last mournful cry and then a change began. In the bear's place stood an Indian dressed in full regalia as an Indian Chief. He was dressed in a white buffalo robe. Standing tall he wore a bear claw necklace around his neck. He had a headdress with eagle feathers on them. It was Ayoka with a set jaw.

Beside Ayoka stood the wolf. The wolf's white hair covered the ground like snow. A dark haired man appeared. It was Frederick! Around his neck was a bear claw necklace, and in his cowboy hat there were eagle feathers. Frederick and Ayoka embraced each other, clasping their hands together in a tight fist and raising them towards the heavens yelling, "blood brothers Forever!" Then they stood in reverent silence. Ayoka's protector and the gods had rewarded them again with their lives. The Cheyenne people bowed down to them, chanting, "Hail Chief Ayoka." Big Blossom, still over by the Chief's teepee was happily smiling.

Chief Many Horses walked over to Ayoka and said, "You have shown our tribe your courage. You have the dignity of a powerful Chief. We have many gifts to send back with you to your tribe." Motioning for Big Blossom, he said, "You have earned my daughter, Big Blossom. Ayoka grimaced.

Chief Big Horn clutched his chest suddenly. He fell to the ground breathing heavily. "Ayoka, come!" he called out in a hoarse voice.

Ayoka had already seen his grandfather fall, and ran over to him. "Grandfather, what is wrong? Looking at the people, he cried, "Get the medicine man, quick!"

"No, my grandson. There is not much time. I designate you to be Chief of the Sioux Tribe. Take my staff from me. You shall be the youngest Chief in the history of the Indian nation."

"No Grandfather, please don't leave. I need you." Ayoka fell to his knees beside him holding his hand.

Chief Big Horn gasping for breath smiled at Ayoka. Then he closed his eyes. There was serenity about him now. He was on his way to the Happy Hunting Ground. Ayoka laid his head on his grandfather's chest and wailed unashamedly. Everyone left but Frederick, his blood brother who lifted his limp body up, putting his arm around him. Big Blossom appeared with tears in her eyes. Looking at Ayoka, she said in a kind voice, "Me sorry! I will help you prepare him for the 'happy hunting ground'!"

CHAPTER 59

PREPARATION FOR THE HAPPY HUNTING GROUND

The trip back to the Sioux Camp was a sad one for Ayoka although he knew that his grandfather had lived a good life. He was an exceptionally good man and a great respected Chief that would never be forgotten

Chief Many Horses had given him and Frederick two magnificent steeds as gifts to ride home. Ayoka pulled a travois with his grandfather on it. Big Blossom walked behind Ayoka the many miles to the Black Hills patiently. Frederick rode one of the steeds behind the procession. The Cheyenne tribe followed them too. The procession was miles long. They trudged along slowly.

When they arrived at the camp the Chief's friends and relatives were waiting to greet them. Many tribes were present. Wee was waiting for them and took them to the campfire where there was food waiting for them. Women were sitting around a campfire rocking back and forth and wailing. While the men and their guests began to eat, Big Blossom and other women took Chief Big Horn to his teepee to prepare him for his trip.

Ayoka told Wee about their trip. She was shocked at the happenings, but she smiled when she noticed Big Blossom waiting on Ayoka hand and foot. Ayoka told her that Chief Many Horses gave her to him for one of his wives, because she had been Pony Boy's wife. Wee knew that this was the custom, but she also knew that Big Blossom was several years older than Ayoka and this was going to pose a problem, because she knew her brother's heart belonged to someone else. She also knew that the spirits would watch over him and solve this problem as they had done in the past.

CHAPTER 60

FREDERICK MAKES HIS MIND UP

Ayoka and Frederick tied their steeds in back of Chief Big Horn's teepee with the rest of his horses. While they were doing this, Kysha came up with Chop Stix. The 'Most Lordly Dog' scampered behind them with his tongue hanging out. Ayoka and Frederick were happy to see their comrades. Gypsy let out a loud whinny and was answered by a squeal. Peeking from behind his mother, there stood a cocky little colt on wobbly legs looking at them. You could tell that his father was Chop Stix. He had that same mischievous glint in his eyes and a speckled rump like Gypsy's. They praised Gypsy and Chop Stix and petted them.

Frederick was happy that Kysha was so thoughtful in bringing their horses and the new arrival. The timing was perfect. The new arrival helped to soothe Ayoka's mind. Looking at the two of them made him realize that Kysha would make Chief Ayoka a good wife. He couldn't help but let out a winded relieved sigh, "Phew!"

Frederick knew that he was far from ready to have a wife and a family. There were more adventures out in the world waiting for him. In no way was he likely to settle down for a long while. That's all he would need, a wife and squalling babies. He wasn't agin the opposite sex, that was for sure, but he wasn't the type to love 'em, marry 'em and leave 'em neither. Nope he sure wasn't ready to get roped into the corral yet. And besides something was lacking in Kysha that he needed in a woman. He couldn't quite put his finger on it. She was an eyeful and full of spunk, but beauty to him wasn't everything.

Ayoka called, "Hey blood brother, what are you brooding about?"

"Oh just about the future, I guess." Frederick mumbled.

CHAPTER 61

PREPARATION FOR SPIRITUAL JOURNEY

The women were busy preparing Chief Big Horn for his journey to the 'Happy Hunting Ground' where there was plenty of game. They put his best decorative warrior clothes on him. His prestigious war bonnet with many eagle feathers covered his head. They hung his medicine bag around his neck."

Ayoka and Wee entered the teepee to bid their grandfather "farewell". Everyone left, so they could be alone with him. Ayoka placed his grandfather's hand on his heart. This was a traditional peace sign. Wee placed a blue ribbon in his hand for good luck on his journey.

Soon the burial ceremony began to take place. Darkness had set in. The fireworks began! The men fired off their thundersticks through the hole left at the top of Chief Big Horn's teepee. As soon as this firing ceased, the old women commenced knocking and making such a rattling at the door to frighten away any spirit that would dare to come near.

After making sure no spirits lingered, they cut birch bark into narrow strips, like ribbons. They folded these pieces into shapes, and hung them inside the teepee, so that the last puff of wind would move them. With such scarecrows as these, the spirits would not disturb their slumbers. They removed his body and took it through the western wall of the house, in the direction of the land of the dead.

The funeral possession took Chief Big Horn to his favorite thinking place. The chosen gravesite was in the mountains among towering trees, where the air was cool and where he had spent many hours during his life. Wild life was abundant here. It was where the bison and elk walked the riverbank. His Palomino horse, Sabine was slain at the gravesite. Now Chief Big Horn would not be left afoot in the spirit land.

The men had already prepared a deep grave. They placed him in it with his head towards the west. By his side they placed his hunting and war implements; his bow and arrow, tomahawk, gun, pipe and tobacco, knife, pouch, flint and steel, medicine-bag, kettle, trinkets and other articles. He would need them on his long journey. Next to him they laid Sabine dressed in finery. On top of his grave they put poles lengthways, to the height of about 2 feet over which birch bark or mats form a covering to secure the body from the rain. His relations and friends sat on the ground in a circle round the head of the grave wailing.

The women under Wee's supervision prepared all kinds of meat, dog soup, and firewater. The food was handed to the people present in bowls, a certain quantity saved for a burnt offering. They saved food for the soul, because it would take a portion, which was consumed by fire.

His best friend, Eagle Man, gave a prayer to the soul of his dear departed friend. He enumerated his good qualities, imploring the blessing of the dead that his Spirit may intercede for them, and they would have lots of game. He told how the Chief served his people faithfully and watched out for their welfare. With his head bowed, he said, "All his life my friend and chief shared his possessions with everyone." Eagle Man also asked his spirit to depart quietly from Big Chief Horn.

When the funeral was over, Ayoka and Wee dispersed many of his belongings to his tribe and friends. All of his fine horses were given away. Ayoka received his prized buffalo horse, a black stallion with white stockings, named Wild One. He was a master in a buffalo hunt.

At the close of the ceremonies, Frederick said, "Blood brother, it is time for me to return to my home with Wee and prepare for her wedding. We will leave in the morning at daybreak. Meanwhile I need to go help Wee pack."

Ayoka shook his head. Frederick would never learn. He always would help the women.

CHAPTER 62

THE MYSTERIOUS RETREAT

Ayoka retreated to the woods thinking deep thoughts. His blood brother would leave in the morning. They had been together for three years now in one adventure after another. Now it was time for both of them to look towards their future and go their separate ways. They had proven themselves as brave courageous boys, but now they were men, and no matter what, who would always be bloodbrothers forever.

He began whittling on a piece of hickory wood. His tribe was without a Chief now legally, and soon the Great Council would have a meeting to make him the leading Chief of the Sioux tribe. He needed to court a woman whom he loved to help rule the tribe with him. A woman who was wise and one who could help him make the right decisions and a woman who would bring him many children. That would be Kysha. He knew there would be other suitors. He had never courted her in the proper way. He wasn't sure about her feelings toward him. She always kept him guessing. Tonight he was going to find out she felt, and soon! This evening if he finished making his elk flute he would go outside her teepee and court her with some fluted love songs. When he saved her from Pony Boy, hadn't she run into his arms? Maybe she would welcome him with her blanket. Ayoka continued working and whittling on the flute. He carved an eagle on it in memory of Goldie. He put six round holes in it. This represented the earth and sky and the four directions; north, south, east and west. The flute was finally ready. Goldie would be pleased with this flute.

CHAPTER 63

THE SECRET ENCOUNTER

Ayoka's ears picked up soft moccasin feet pitter-pattering down the path. He jumped behind a bush. It was Kysha. She was coming to fill the water jugs. He placed the 'wind that breathes life into the heart' into his mouth. A melody filled the air sounding like a nightingale and falling waters.

She filled her water jugs and sat them down on the ground. Then she sat down with her slender legs bent under her and rocked back and forth to his music, closing her eyes. She began to hum. She opened her eyes and raked her fingers through the lush grass beside her as if looking for something. Ayoka knew what she was looking for. It was called gamma grass. The lucky in love grass. She found the bloom and put it in her hair and looked towards the bush where he was. She smiled teasingly.

He made the flute sing with passion." After awhile, she picked up the water jugs, and with lithesome grace she glided up the path as if she were in a dream. He had a strong desire to catch her in his arms again and kiss those ruby red lips until she couldn't catch her breath. He wasn't a patient man.

Before he could come from the bushes, he heard heavy footsteps coming down to the river's edge. A voice called out, "Ayoka. Oh there you are. We need to talk before I leave in the morning." It was Frederick.

"Yes we need to talk blood brother," Ayoka said as he tucked the flute in his belt and sat down on the grass.

Frederick sat down beside him with his chin resting on his knees. "I saw Kysha. She passed me as if she didn't see me. What did you do to her?"

Ignoring Frederick's question, Ayoka said, "By the time we meet again, maybe many moons will be past. I will be Chief of my tribe with many problems concerning our land and our Indian heritage's future. What are your plans for the future, my blood brother? Are you going to settle down and get married?

"Get married. Are you kidding? Your guess is as good as mine, Ayoka. There's this constant hunger for adventure that never leaves my mind to be a part of the unknown." Hesitating, he said. "The last thing I'm thinking about is marriage. What woman would want to be married to a man who longs for the wide-open spaces? It just wouldn't be fair to her. And besides I haven't seen any woman that I want to spend the rest of my life with, and that makes me glad. Didn't you ever wonder what's going on in the rest of the world, over the mountains Ayoka?" Not waiting for an answer, he said, "I aim to find out!" Looking at his blood brother, whose forehead was wrinkled and worried, he asked, "What's the matter my blood brother?"

Ayoka remained silent for a long time. Glancing towards the setting sun, he began talking, "I worry about my Indian tribe's future. I worry about the disappearance of the buffalo, which my people have to have to live on to survive. I worry about the gold that the palefaces are seeking and invading our lands for. Our freedom is slowly being taken away, and your government is talking about putting us on reservations.

Frederick butted in saying, "But Ayoka, the Black Hills are sacred, and they belong to you."

"The palefaces have broken all treaties between us so far. Why do you think they will keep the promises that the Black Hills are ours forever?" He took hold of Frederick's hand. "I wish things could stay as they are now brother, our friendship, our free plains, the buffalo, and land."

Frederick butted in again. "Nothing will ever kill our relationship, blood brother. Nothing!"

"Nothing Frederick? And what if your big Chief of the palefaces wants you to join the soldiers to fight us, Frederick? Then what will you do? Turn against your own country?"

Frederick interrupted him, "My country, Ayoka? You mean God's land and your land!" Frederick didn't know how to answer. America had been good to his father and him. He was troubled. "Just remember brother, I will always be there for you."

"And me for you." Ayoka's lips were drawn in a straight firm line. With darkened eyes, he said in a hoarse voice, "blood brothers Forever Frederick!"

Clasping hands and raising their clenched fist upward, they both were wondering if this vowel would ever be broken. The sun had gone down, and a full moon hung over the mountains. If they had noticed the face of the moon, they would have seen the face of a buffalo flooded with tears.

They turned in for the night, but Ayoka and Frederick both lay awake for a long time. Their thoughts were the same. Frederick was thinking about the Indian's situation. And Ayoka was worried about the plight of his people.

CHAPTER 64

THE WEDDING DRESS

The next morning Ayoka had made up his mind that life had to go on. He was going courting. He cleaned up, slicking his black hair down with bear grease. Then he picked up his flute and headed to Kysha's teepee. He saw her mother peeking out the window. He played 'Won't You Come Out Tonight' and other melodies. Soon Kysha came out of the door carrying a blanket. Ayoka was already sitting down. She crept over to him, throwing the blanket over both of them. They huddled together whispering. He finally said, "Kysha, I'd like you to share my teepee with me. I've thought a lot about it lately. I want you for my wife."

"Oh, Ayoka, yes someday I'd like you for my man, but I'm not ready right now. I care for you, but I am not ready to settle down with babies. After many moons pass I might be ready to take on the duties of a wife of a Chief of the Sioux tribe." She asked mischievously, "Will you wait for me?"

Angrily, Ayoka jumped up, jerking the blanket off of them. His dark eyes snapped. "Don't tease around with me, Kysha. Does it make a difference that I am not Chief now?" His voice was full of scorn. He didn't wait for an answer. "I don't have time to wait for you to grow up."

Her full lips puffed out into a pout. Ayoka grabbed her, pulling her tightly to him. She struggled a little. He put one hand on her head tipping it up to him. He pressed his lips to hers. She tried to resist him, but a delicious feeling flooded her body, and before she knew it, she was kissing him back. She knew at that moment that she would be his until the end of time. Just as she was enjoying the moment, he released her abruptly.

In a husky voice, he said, "I will not be one of your toys. When you've grown up, then come to me, if it's not too late!" He jerked his flute from his belt. He snapped it in half and threw it down. "This will be the last time I will make a fool out of myself for any woman." He turned abruptly and left.

She burst out sobbing and ran into her teepee and threw herself down on her bed. Her mother came over to soothe her, saying, "You and Ayoka going to get married? I need to know when, so your wedding dress will be ready."

She raised her tear stained face up and said, "Mother, he's not going to ask me again to marry him! He thinks I need to grow up."

Her mother rubbed her back until she fell asleep. Covering her up with a light blanket, she walked into the center of the large room where the blazing fire was making flickering shadows on the wall. She picked up the white buffalo skin and getting the awl out she began sewing on the wedding dress.

Her husband took out his pipe, and puffed on it. He winked at her and said. "When is the wedding going to be wife?"

She smiled knowingly, saying, "When the chill is out of the air my husband." Then she winked back at him.

Ayoka paced back and forth on the floor of his teepee. Women could sure stir men up. He knew Kysha had been brought up to be a dutiful and obedient daughter whenever her father gave her definite commands. He knew that she was young, tender hearted and romantic. But she wasn't going to play with his heartstrings. He was an Indian brave that played for keeps! When he had her in his arms, he wanted to take her away with him to his teepee and make her his wife, but she would have to learn that he would be the boss. Right now he didn't have time to think about women.

A Council delegation was meeting in the morning. The people of his tribe wanted to make him the Chief. Right now he was too tired to think about it. He had to clear his mind. Women!

CHAPTER 65

LIFE GOES ON

Wee and Frederick headed out towards their ranch without stopping to tell Ayoka "Goodbye". Wee brought Big Blossom with them. As they were riding through the prairie, she gave Frederick some more news. Otto and Jake had built a trading post along the Oregon Trail. This would provide a rest stop for immigrants. Frederick was excited at this news, thinking that he might get to help with this new venture of theirs.

THE YOUNGEST INDIAN CHIEF EVER

Many moons passed, and now it was two years later. Ayoka had grown into a young macho man who was now Chief of the Sioux Tribe. He ruled with an iron hand. Not only did he understand the needs of his Indian brothers; he met the white man as a brother, through his association with Frederick. He was known throughout the land and his own tribe as being noble, wise, brave and truehearted.

After accepting the title of Chief, his friend, Bold One and he worked diligently through the spring making his own teepee. His teepee was the largest in the camp. It took several white buffalo skins to cover the poles. Kysha and her young maiden friends brought their awls and sinew, sewing diligently. She had turned down many suitors, trying to prove to Ayoka that she was waiting for him. She seemed to have grown up somewhat. He was stubborn and was waiting until she came to him with the blanket.

Bold One supervised the covering around the poles, pinning them together with wooden pegs. The fireplace was in the middle of the teepee, with a hole at the top for a chimney. The door of the teepee faced east to greet the sun. Across from the door was the place of honor for guests. The older women of the camp worked hard making backrest chairs out of willow. There was a sleeping area covered with buffalo robes. Against the walls were containers and bags used for storing food, clothing and his personal belongings.

Ayoka could not wait to decorate the outside of his teepee with drawings and symbols of his vision and adventures with Frederick. But he was not an artist, and this teepee was to be special. Frederick acquainted him with a famous artist who depicted the Western and Indian culture. His name was George Catlin.

"This man is a true friend of the Indians," Frederick told him. He had met him at his Pa's and Unk's trading post. For payment the artist only wanted to learn the culture and history of the Indians and to be able to paint pictures of the ways of the Indians. He was truly interested in the Indian's welfare. Ayoka sent for him.

Artist Catlin listened to Ayoka as he told parts of his life, thus far. He worked many moons painting scenes on Ayoka's teepee, and the Indians always gathered around and watched him with absorbed interest.

A huge white buffalo with two boys on its back was painted on the sides of the teepee. Pinnacle Mountain was painted in the background with Goldie hovering over it. Over the doorway there was a large moon with the face of a buffalo on it. It was very awesome. At the completion of the artwork, Mr. Catlin asked Ayoka if he could go on a planned buffalo hunt with the hunters. Ayoka was very pleased with this interest and let him ride one of the best buffalo horses in the tribe. Mr. Catlin painted the scene later. He was amazed that some buffalo stood six feet tall. Before he departed, Ayoka gave him many gifts, and as he was leaving, Ayoka took his hand and said, "Sha-sha (means very red and the work was unique and excellent). Ayoka's teepee only needed one more thing now. That was a woman for his wife. He intended to remedy that situation once and for all soon.

CHAPTER 67

THE PROPOSAL

One day while feeding his many horses, and taking them down to the river for water, he noticed Chop Stix' little mule son frolicking about. He had turned out to be a handsome little mule with a sassy attitude like his mother. Ayoka held out some berries, and he pranced up gingerly taking them with his lips. Ayoka said to Chop Stix who had trotted up, "It's time to name your little son, Chop Stix." He hawed in agreement. "I know just the name for you, little mule, he said. Let's call you AyFred." Then he put a rope around AyFred's neck, leading him up the path to a grassy area. He tethered him there. He had plans for this little mule.

Kysha had shown him in little ways that she was ready to settle down. He would give her one more chance to become his wife. If she teased him again and turned him down, he would ask another one of the maidens who were always vying for his attentions.

Behind his teepee were many horses, which Ayoka had acquired through raids and as gifts. Like his grandfather, Ayoka had given many horses away. He chose eight of his best horses, putting them aside. Whistling, he began grooming them. He led them over to Kysha's tent. He knew that she was not there. The door was open. Ayoka picketed the horses. Then he walked into the tent.

Kysha's mother was very happy and honored to have Chief Ayoka come visit. Her husband, who was smoking his pipe as usual, asked Ayoka to sit down. Ayoka sat down. He waited for Kysha's father; to speak first as young people showed respect that way. After awhile, he said, "Why are we honored with your visit Chief Ayoka?"

Ayoka said, "I have brought you many horses. I want to make Kysha my wife." They got up and walked out the door to look them. The father was pleased over the sleek horses, but Kysha would have to accept Ayoka's proposal, before he could accept them. They parted amicably.

CHAPTER 68

THE TAMING OF AYOKA'S WOMAN

The evening was an exceptional warm night with the Chinook wind blowing lazily over the camp. He went to the door as he always did after eating to look out over the camp. He saw a figure approaching his teepee, wrapped in a blanket. He couldn't believe it. It was Kysha. Girls just didn't do this. The man always went to her teepee. He walked out silently to meet her. The tribal people were gaping at this unusual ritual, but knowing Kysha they knew she would do the unexpected. Taking the initiative she threw the blanket over his head. Still standing, she pulled his head down to hers brushing his lips teasingly with her tongue. Then throwing the blanket off of them, she pulled away from him, running towards the river. She yelled over her shoulder. "Catch me if you can Chief Ayoka."

She sped down the curving path to the river with the grace of a deer. Ayoka, his heart thumping, raced close behind her. The full moon was bright. He almost caught her, but she slipped away. Nearing the river with the singing waterfall, he tripped over a limb, but made a dive catching her as he fell.

As he held her close lying on the soft mossy ground smothering her with kisses, she whispered, "Now I have you. I will marry you Chief Ayoka, but there will be no other wives. Ever! Okay? Promise me, or I will marry someone who only wants one wife." Ayoka sought her lips again, but she turned them away. "Promise, that I will be the only woman for you."

The sound of the waterfall roared as it tumbled down from a high cliff. He whispered in her ear, "I promise my untamed one. You will be the only one for me! But only if you promise that you will come to my teepee to live. I will not move to yours." She turned her lips close to his again, but he turned away. "You're teasing with me again sweet one to get your own way. Promise me! I shall be the boss of my woman and we shall live happily ever after in my teepee!"

Now the tradition of the Indians was that when a couple got married, the man moved into the girl's teepee, bringing gifts to the family. Ayoka had built his teepee to his specifications, and in no way did he want to live with the in-laws. If she accepted his proposal, this change would be a first in his camp or any other camp.

She pouted. "That is not the tradition, Ayoka. Mother and father would not be happy about that arrangement. I don't want our marriage to start out on bad medicine."

"Remember I am the head of our house. There will be no bad medicine. I will speak to your father. All will be well cautious one!"

She began singing, "I promise, I prom..." He gave no heed to her finishing her song. His lips quieted her. She was going to be his woman, his only woman. And he would be the boss of his teepee! There was no need for more words.

CHAPTER 69

THE UNWELCOME ONE

Frederick, Wee, and Big Blossom had a good trip back to the ranch. When they got there, the oil lamp was flickering in the window. Otto met them at the door, because he had heard the pounding of horse hooves coming.

Frederick lifted Wee down and took the horses to the barn. Wee ran to Otto's open arms. Following her was Big Blossom with her head down. Jake was there with Otto, and they had been playing cards. In the excitement of being home, they forgot all about Big Blossom, who walked over the fireplace and in Indian fashion, sat down on the floor, cross-legged. Her face was sad.

Big Jake walked over to where she was, and in a booming voice said, "What have we here?"

Big Blossom covered her face. Big Blossom could not speak English, and she was afraid of men. Everything got very quiet.

Wee began telling them the story of Frederick's and Ayoka's latest adventure. She said Big Blossom was given to Ayoka to become his wife. When Wee went to leave, Big Blossom wanted to come with her. Pony Boy had abused her, and she was frightened of most men. She told Wee that she would help her with the household chores, and she would sleep outside if she would take her home with her. Wee felt sorry for her and brought her along.

Big Jake, still standing and looking at Big Blossom, with his mustache twitching grabbed her by the hand and yanked her up facing him. He scrutinized her with his cool eyes. This big man with yellow hair frightened her even more. Noticing a cross around her neck with the markings of the Blackfeet

Tribe, in Indian tongue, his big voice shook the cabin. "You are of the Blackfeet Tribe, aren't you?"

She nodded her head back and forth, meaning no.

He shoved her away abruptly and stormed out of the door. He was taller than the door, and as he was going out, he forgot to duck and hit his head.

Otto had never seen his friend act this way, and he had never hit his head on that doorway before. Otto said, "What in the tarnation is wrong with him? He's acting like a mule with a burr under his tail."

As Wee consoled Big Blossom, he said. "Don't worry, I'll discuss this with him. Under these circumstances, he will not be welcome in our home anymore!"

Big Jake didn't come down the mountain for a long time. Big Blossom was a big help to Wee. She helped make her wedding dress. She was very neat in her sewing, and had brought several pearl beads, which she planned to adorn the dress with. Wee showed her how to fix her stringy hair into a neat braided bun. They also began making her some clothes. Instead of the dowdy looking rags she had worn, she now had buckskin pants and dresses and fringed skirts. Wee noticed that when she wore these new clothes, she had a nice curved figure. When she smiled, which was seldom, the whole room would light up, and she was almost pretty.

CHAPTER 70

A DISCOVERY

Big Jake came down from his cave one morning, acting as if nothing was wrong. He didn't know that Otto, Frederick and Wee had gone to town to the trading post. When he walked in the cabin door, Big Blossom was in the kitchen making Indian coffee. Big Jake sat down at the table watching her in complete silence. She no longer had the necklace on. Without speaking, she walked over to the table and placed a hot steaming cup of coffee before him. She had stirred up some cornpone, which she sat by his cup.

"Humph!" He looked at her scowling. He sipped the coffee slowly, watching every move she made. Then he took a bite of the cornpone. "Ummmm." Looking at her, he said, "you sure 'nough can cook even if you are a Blackfoot Injun!"

She walked over to him and took his hat from his head. He grabbed his head with both hands, looking up at her with startled eyes. He said, "Yer ain't fixin to scalp me, are ya Blackfoot woman?" His expression was distrustful. Reaching up he grabbed her small hands covering them completely with his large hands and held them tightly.

Big Blossom put her hands on her hips and raised her voice saying, "Me no Blackfoot woman, me Cheyenne!" Then speaking softly, she said, "Me think hair is pretty." He loosened her hands. She ran her fingers through his long yellow tangled hair. "Pretty! Needs bath though." she exclaimed.

Now nobody ever called Big Jake "pretty." He jumped up from the table, grabbed his beaver cap, slammed it on his head and headed for the door. She covered her mouth with her hand not wanting him to hear giggles escape her lips. But he heard them. Thinking she was making fun at him, he turned looking like a burly bear ready to attack. But then staring at her in complete dismay, with cold penetrating eyes, his expression softened. She was looking at him smiling. Her dark eyes showed merriment. It lit up the whole room, changing her entire face. In an outburst, he bellowed out, "Dadburn, if you ain't the prettiest Injun woman I've ever seen." By this time he was embarrassed. Rushing out he bumped his head on that doggoned door again. Taking long strides he shot up the mountain at a quickened pace. That night he was restless. He had not felt this way since his woman had been killed by those dadblamed unprincipled Blackfeet Indians. He lay awake for hours. He couldn't get that lovely smile off his mind. Soon he relaxed all his muscles and went into a deep slumber. The next morning when he woke up and walked to the mouth of his cave, there was a whole basket of cornpones by his door.

Big Blossom hummed a song as she cleaned up the cabin. That big strong man was something to look at and so gentle. Big Blossom was not used to kind men. She decided right there and then that living with Wee and Otto was the best thing that had ever happened to her.

CHAPTER 71

BORDER FEVER

Frederick had gown into a handsome young man. The restless spirit that seemed to be born in him never left. He still had a wild craving for adventure. The wildness in him could be a detriment or an early death. .

After parting with Ayoka, he began working as a clerk at his Pa's and Unk's trading post. All kinds of people traveling westward on the Oregon Trail stopped there for various items they would need to set up and work their homesteads. Looking at the prairie always showed a steady stream of families in creaking, covered wagons heading westward. Usually Indians could be seen watching them from a cliff or mountain.

Fur trade and timber had become the most important activity in the region. Jake and Big Blossom had become great friends. Jake found out that the Cheyenne tribe had a skirmish with the Blackfoot tribe. The Blackfoot tribe kidnapped Big Blossom. One night she stole away going back to her grandfather's tribe. The Blackfoot Injuns had given her the necklace with their emblem. Big Jake was happy that she was Cheyenne. They hunted together and kept the post supplied with many furs.

Lately there were meetings with Otto and Jake with military personnel. They were interested in buying their trading post and making a military post out of it.

Otto was very patriotic and his heart was full of love for America. He always said that America had given him so much that he wanted to give something back to it and was willing to sell it to them. He no longer had the time to work in the garden with Wee, and they were not spending as much time together as they wished.

Big Jake liked America too, but he also realized that it took cold cash to make ends meet. And besides he and Big Blossom had become much more than close friends. She could hunt better than most men, and liked the wilderness as much as he did. She was spending more time in his cave than she was with Wee. He began thinking of a homestead with a log home on it and putting a ring on Big Blossom's finger. So selling the trading post was a possibility in the minds of both Otto and Jake.

CHAPTER 72

THE TRADING POST

Many moons had passed since the days Ayoka and Frederick had first met. Also changes were occurring in their lives. Ayoka was Chief of the Sioux Tribe, and he and Kysha were married. They now had twin sons, plus Ayoka had given her AyFred as part of her wedding gifts.

Otto and Wee were married now. Frederick had met many girls through working at the trading post and attending church, but no girl made his heart have the strong emotional feeling that others in love seemed to have. There was an emptiness and restlessness in him, which could not be satisfied.

Through his job of clerking at the trading post, he met people of all trades and nationalities; gold rushers, mountain men, hunters, trappers, settlers, and immigrants coming in their store from all over the country. There were friendly Indians who shadowed out of the forest to barter and visit. If soldiers were present, the Indians were stalked. Frederick did not approve of this.

Everyone had a story to tell, and Frederick could never hear enough about their colorful tales. The stories some of these people told stirred his imagination. Many hours were spent around the pot-bellied stove telling how the Indians had attacked them, how some of them had struck gold in the hills and how they had met the big Grizzly and lived to tell about it.

Many changes were occurring now. News traveled fast with eager to talk people who stopped at their Post. The Pony Express carriers stopped there, exchanging their tired horses for fresh ones and rushing to their destinations on time. Soldiers badgered Frederick to join them in their skirmishes with the

Indians. It was a mystery to them why Frederick wasn't interested. One day a soldier made the mistake of saying, "Are you an Injun Lover?"

Later the man said, "I didn't know what hit me." Frederick didn't have any trouble with these questions anymore. A civil war was brooding between the north and the south. A railroad had been built through the prairie and it was fascinating to see 'the big Iron Horse (as the Indians called it) chugging along. The Indians were very much alarmed at this.

When Frederick wasn't working he explored every streams, valleys and mountains in the area. He was absolutely fearless. He had learned many things and was known as an excellent woodsman through his association with his blood brother, Ayoka and Unk Jake.

CHAPTER 73

THE MEETING

One day a German Immigrant girl came into the store quite frustrated. Frederick was standing on a ladder busy stocking the shelves, when he felt a light tug on his pant leg. Turning his head around and looking down, he looked into the tear filled greenest eyes that he had ever seen. He became weak and his head began to spin. Missing a step on the ladder, he lost his balance stumbling to the floor. Excusing himself as he bumped against her, he was memorized. Her silky golden hair fell in waves below her shoulders. Why she was the most beautiful woman looking gal he had ever seen. He began to stutter, which was unusual for bold Frederick. "Can, can I...I help you M'am?" He had never seen her in these parts before.

Her smile was that of an angel, and she had a deep dimple on the right side of her cheek. In a broken foreign accent and peaking from under a large sun-bonnet, she said, "Hard for me to talk English, but Vater (father) and wagen (wagon) broke down. Fraulein needs helefn! (help)"

The tears made her eyes greener, and he just stood there with a dumb-founded look on his face staring at her for minutes without answering. He was thinking back to the picture of his mother on the fireplace at the cabin. Why she looked just like her. She had the same softness and sweetness about her facial features.

She looked at him questionably, "Understand?" she asked with her lips quivering. Frederick was never at a loss for words, but her innocent beauty and fragile helpfulness overpowered him.

Then he realized that some of the words she was saying were in German. He picked up a few German words from his Pa, but just a little. Now he could kick himself for not learning his motherland language now. He continued to stare at this dream of a girl in a simple green calico dress. It complimented her slender body and those eyes. As he racked his brain for some German words that he could remember, he said. "Sprechen Deutsche Fraulein? (Do you speak German Miss?) He stooped down to hear her answer.

Joyfully she cried "Ja! Ja!" (meaning yes, yes) as her face broke into a happy smile. She was so pleased that someone knew her language.

Otto was in the trading post that day. Frederick called to him telling him that he would need to take some tools to help these people with their broken down wagon. Otto was so happy that he could talk to someone who was from the old country. He smiled knowingly, winking at him, saying to him in English, "Ahhhhh Frederick. You are taken with this Fraulein." This was an understatement of the year.

CHAPTER 74

TWITTERPATED

While Frederick was getting some tools Otto gave her a drink of hot chocolate and had her sit down while she waited. When he returned, she watched every move Frederick made with an open innocence. What muscular arms he had. He is so strong, she thought.

He felt her eyes watching him. Frederick turned his red face towards the shelves, packing a few tools in a gunnysack. He also took some wagon wheels. Going outside, he hitched Gypsy to a wagon. Then loading it with the supplies he tethered her pony to the back of it. Putting his hands around the girl's small waist, he lifted her upon the wagon seat. He felt as if he were handling a piece of Dresden china.

Most of the ride was in silence. They did not talk much because of communication. Other heavy wagons creaked by, and horses neighed at one another. Their occupants waved at them. He would point to the beauty of the mountains on the prairie and exchange glances with her now and then. She folded her hands in her lap. He could feel her studying him. She felt an excitement tickling inside of her of just being close to him. The smell of the dessert sage and the brush of the air blowing her hair made her feel at ease with this man. Oh, if she could only communicate with him and find out all about him. About two miles down the prairie was their prairie schooner (covered wagon) with a broken axle.

Her father had fallen asleep and his spectacles lay on the ground. He woke up with a start at the sound of the rattling wagon feeling his eyes realizing he had lost his glasses. Frederick reined the horses to a halt. He jumped off the wagon with one bound and picked the old man's glasses up and handed to them, saying, "Sir you might need these." He turned and gently lifted this dream of a girl off the wagon.

The man adjusted them on his face and in English said, "Thanks young man! In no way could I continue our trip with out my bifocals." He was very happy that his daughter had brought help. Frederick learned that they were headed to her aunt's homestead about 10 more miles down the plains. Frederick quickly fixed the broken axle.

Her father wanted to pay Frederick. "Name it boy, I will pay you for fixing our wagon."

Frederick looked past her father saying; "I must see your daughter again! That will be my payment."

He translated Frederick's statement to her. So he wasn't taken, she thought. She lowered her lashes. Her father said, "It's up to her lad." She raised her eyes and looked long into Frederick's eyes. Her open innocence appealed to him. She did not try to be coy or giddy. Her silence did not dampen his spirit. That only gave him time to look at her.

She reached out her small hand to him and when he clasped it gently, he felt something soft in it. He held on to her hand, not wanting to let it go. She melted him. He was putty in her hands.

As they readied to go, Frederick noticed Indians watching from a steep cliff down the prairie. He warned them that if any Indians approached them to mention his name, and tell them that they were friends of Frederick of the trading post. The father thanked him and with a loud "Git Up," they headed on their journey. Frederick watched them until they were small specks and out of sight. Then he opened his sweaty clenched hand, which he had forgotten about. There was a beautiful lacy handkerchief folded. Inside was a picture of her encased in a neatly folded note. It was written in German. He folded the note back in the handkerchief and slipped it inside his shirt where it lay against his heart. Jumping on Gypsy he raced back to the post. They skidded to a stop. Running inside, he pulled his Pa aside.

Otto said, "What's the matter son?"

Breathlessly Frederick said, "Quick Pa." Reaching in his shirt he pulled the note out handing it to Otto. "Read it to me Pa. It's in German." As Otto read the note, Frederick held the picture of this down to earth lovely girl in his hand gazing at her.

Otto read the note in a soft voice, "My name is Katrina Krek. Everyone calls me Kat. My heart will ache until I see my knight in shining armor again."

Frederick broke into a run through the post, out the door. Like a young colt he leapt into the air, throwing his hat whirling it high into the air and yelling. "Yes, yes, yes!" People stopped and looked at this wild maniac getting out of his way.

She wasn't like the other girls Frederick had flirted with. He could take them for awhile or leave them. A woman like her was dangerous without realizing it. She was a woman that was an open book. He wanted to protect and take care of her. What was wrong with him? Was he going soft? He would see her again. He would find her. That was for sure!

As Katrina and her father rolled along in the ruts of other wagons, she knew that Frederick would always be on her mind. He was so rugged and yet so handsome, but a sizzling wildness in him had stirred her senses. Better yet, he was from Germany. It would take a strong woman to capture and tame him. And strong she wasn't. Would she ever see him again in this desolate place? He had said that he must see her again. She hoped so, but how and when?

CHAPTER 75

THE SURPRISE VISITOR

Several months later a distinguished uniformed man walked into the trading post with a paper in his hand. Although he was not very old, is hair was maturely white and he had a well-trimmed mustache. He had an Army uniform on and his jacket was covered with medals.

There was a board that hung on the wall where announcements could be posted. He put a long sheet of paper on it with a heading of 'Men Wanted for the Lady Franklin Bay Expedition.' Frederick was curious as to who he was and what this expedition was all about.

The man noticed the young boyish man's curiosity and identified himself as Lieutenant Greely, an Army man. He explained to Frederick that there was going to be a government expedition in a faraway land, a land that was frozen with petrified mountains. The expedition was called the Lady Franklin Bay. Frederick immediately asked what the purpose of the expedition was. They would be performing scientific exploration, such as weather conditions, etc., and would be gone for two years, the man explained. Frederick had never heard of such a land, but he was thirsting for more information. He offered him some coffee, and as they weren't busy he asked him to sit for a spell and tell him all about this place. Lieutenant Greely was glad to satisfy the young man's unquenchable hunger for information about this adventure. It was a virgin land that had never been fully discovered he told Frederick. He described the land as being abundant with strange looking animals. It was a land, so appalling and dangerous that the men who went on this expedition might not come back alive. After he told Frederick this, he thought, if this man is cowardly, he won't think anymore about this venture.

Lt. Greeley was looking for 26 young men to accompany him to this land. It would be a dangerous undertaking, and only the fittest young men should apply. Frederick was excited. He was ready to prepare for the journey. But there was only one stipulation that would hold Frederick back. The expedition was composed of enlisted men only. Lieutenant Greely told Frederick that the complete details of the expedition would be coming soon, and if he was interested, he needed to enlist immediately.

This was the answer to Frederick's dreams. His life had been filled with adventures, but little did he realize that none of his previous adventures would stand out as this experience in the far North would. Visions of faraway lands that had never been explored were filling his mind. He was so fascinated by this man and the possible opportunity to be a part of the Lady Franklin Bay Expedition that he couldn't wait to leave the post that night and go home with the news. Lieutenant Greely was impressed with this man. He had a strong feeling that they would meet again.

CHAPTER 76

EVEN DEATH WILL NEVER PART US

There was considerable unrest with the Indians now. Frederick hadn't seen his blood brother for awhile, but knew that he was excelling as a prominent leader in the Sioux resistance to the encroachment of palefaces in the mineral-rich Black Hills. This didn't surprise him at all. So far Chief Ayoka had been able to keep intruders away from The Black Hills, but according to the Indians coming to the Post, something was going on within the Indian Council, a serious undertaking. The palefaces had killed buffalo by the hundreds and leaving their carcasses lying on the desert. This was a great waste to the Indians, as they used every part of the buffalo for their living, and if this killing did not stop, they would soon be facing starvation. Skirmishes were more rampant among the Indians and the palefaces now.

Before Frederick could make a decision of joining the Army, he had to talk to his blood brother, Ayoka. When he got back to the cabin that night, he told his Pa and Wee that he was leaving in a couple of days for Ohio to enlist in the regular army. He said that the only obstacle in this new to be adventure was joining the Army and having to fight the Indians. Otto was proud of his son who loved America as he did. He realized that America was in the midst of many wars, but knew that Frederick had to satisfy his longing for adventure, and this scientific expedition would help make America even a better place to live.

Wee said that Ayoka would understand him joining the military, so he could eventually go on the expedition to the far north. He would not want to stand in Frederick's way.

Frederick politely listened to her, but he knew that the honorable thing to do was meet with Ayoka before he made this important decision. This was strictly a man's business.

That night Frederick sent a message by smoke signals to Ayoka telling him he was on his way to meet with him. The next morning Frederick left on his journey. Everywhere along the prairie, Frederick saw Indian scouts and the Blue Coats. On the distant hill Frederick saw Ayoka. He came galloping down to the prairie with Wolf following. The blood brothers jumped off their horses embracing each other heartily. Ayoka was in complete warhead dress with dangling scalps on his belt.

That night Ayoka, Kysha, and their twin sons in their cradleboards gathered around the campfire. Many of the Indian warriors discussed their war exploits, showing off their scalps they had taken from the paleface soldiers. Ayoka watched Frederick who had an ashen look on his face. After eating and catching up on each other's lives, everyone left for their teepee to get a good night's rest. Kysha bid Frederick farewell with a kiss on the cheek and took her sleeping boys to the teepee. Now the blood brothers were alone. Frederick was still chewing on a piece of cold venison in deep thought.

In a forlorn voice, Ayoka spoke. "My tribe will soon be facing starvation with the palefaces killing the buffalo." Then he remained silent for a long time. "The Great Father in Washington wants to buy the Black Hills and send our people to reservations. We have refused. Now he wants us to let the miners come and dig all the yellow metal up from our hills, then we can have our land back again." Jumping up he said, "How stupid do they think we are Frederick? And now I have heard that a longhaired chief is going to invade our Black Hills." His eyes seethed with fierce anger. He continued saying; "In no way will I sell my people's souls and their heritage. This is our land, and we will fight for it until death."

Leaning forward he put his hand on Ayoka's shoulder in a brief gesture of feeling and reassurance. Speaking passionately in a hoarse voice, Frederick said, "My blood brother. I am heavyhearted over the fighting and bloodshed between our peoples. I have stayed out of the Army, because I did not want to be a part of these killing fields. But I have a chance to go on an expedition to the far North. They are choosing only military men. Until the expedition is formed, this will mean that I will be involved in fighting the Indians…your people…my people…my tribe." His eyes were sad and full of remorse.

Ayoka said, "Remember the vowel we made to one another many moons ago?"

Frederick said, "Yes, I remember, how could I forget."

They sat before the dancing fire, their eyes fixed on it, and each lost in deep thought. In a stolid voice, Ayoka said, "blood brother, you and I have no choice. It is your duty to fight to protect your people and your country. I too have had to fight the palefaces for our land for the many broken treaties and for their sport of killing the buffalo. In order not to be killed I have killed many of your people." He fingered the scalps on his belt. Then looking at Frederick he said, "I've had a vision of a war between the Sioux and the Palefaces. In my vision I saw palefaces lying dead all over the ground. I hope you will not be one of them."

A knot of fear grew tight in Frederick's chest.

Then Ayoka sprang to his feet shouting. "Go my blood brother! Go on with your life." His voice rose echoing throughout the camp. "Do what you have to do. No matter what is written in the stars, we shall remain blood brothers forever! Even death shall not part us!"

Frederick jumped up grabbing Ayoka's hand and raising it with his in clenched fists towards. In unison they cried, "blood brothers Forever!" Then they embraced each other, knowing in their hearts that the future looked mighty bleak. They clung together for a long time, both knowing that they might never see one another again. A full moon was shining. It was the sad face of 'The Great Protector'.

Frederick left early the next morning, knowing that there would be lots of turmoil and bloodshed in the months to come between their peoples.

CHAPTER 77

FREDERICK ENLISTS IN THE ARMY

After Frederick left to enlist in the Army, Otto and Jake decided to sell their trading post to the government for a fair price. This made Wee and Big Blossom so happy. Now they would have time to enjoy their men. Otto was happy that he was helping the America that had been so good to him. Big Jake thought they had practically given their going business away.

The Government immediately made their purchase into a military post. It became one of the most important posts in the history of the wars against the central plains Indians. It gave protection and refreshment to the throngs of people who made the great western migration over the Oregon Trail. It continued to be a station for the Pony Express and the Overland Stage.

Frederick enlisted in the Calvary and was transferred to Ft. Ellis, Missouri where he was assigned to Troop L, of the Second Cavalry.

Ayoka became known as the greatest and youngest chief of the Sioux nation. He and his people refused to go on a reservation. Army troops attacked their camp time and time again, but Chief Ayoka was victorious in all battles. Frederick was always inwardly glad that Ayoka was not killed. He knew that the Indians were outnumbered, and he dreaded the final outcome.

Frederick fought in various Indian campaigns, under a general called Bear Coat, who tried to be fair with the Indians and keep the treaties. This did not make him very popular with the officials in Washington, but it did make a good impression on Frederick. Out of this experience in the Army, he made a good friend, called Brainard. Then a catastrophe occurred. Now Chief Ayoka was in big, big trouble.

Chief Ayoka and his people joined the Cheyenne and other tribes in a battle at the Little Bighorn. It was the vision Ayoka had mentioned to Frederick. There were thousands of Indians and only 250 bluecoats. All of the soldiers were killed along with the nation's beloved hero, Lt. Col. General Custer. America was outraged over the mass killing and demanded revenge from the President of the United States. General Bear Coat was planning retaliation against Ayoka's tribe, and Frederick would be part of it. But then luck intervened, and the momentous period of Frederick's life arrived just in time. Arrangements were finally being made for the Lady Franklin Bay Expedition to the Polar Regions. Ayoka had said that he hoped his blood brother would not be one of the dead Blue Coats in his vision, and Frederick, if chosen, would not be fighting the Indians anymore.

The Government was anxious that no men except those physically perfect should be members of this expedition. A careful search was made of the men who were in the service. Rigid physical examinations were held. Private Frederick immediately volunteered for the expedition, impelled by his love of adventure, and was accepted as a physically perfect man. He was highly recommended and had passed a strict medical examination. His long and hazardous adventures on the western frontier had inured him to the dangers, hardships, and exposure to the hot and bitterly cold plains. These happenings developed in him the quality of helpfulness that would be so essential in Arctic service.

CHAPTER 78

THE CELEBRATION

It was July 4, 1881 and the twenty-six men who had been chosen for the expedition were in high spirits as they prepared for their journey to the North. They would be sailing from St. John's, Newfoundland, July 7, 1881 on the Proteus boat, a sealer of 467 tons. They would remain in the Arctic for two years.

But tomorrow there was going to be a big Fourth of July celebration, celebrating America's fifth anniversary. It would be a celebration that no one would ever forget, because Lt. Greely and his chosen men for the Arctic expedition would be the honored guests. Several dignitaries were going to attend this party. Special invitations to the party were sent to the men's families. Frederick was so excited because his father and Wee were coming to see him before he left. Not only that, they had written him a letter telling him that they were bringing a surprise for him. They would be attending the dinner and the dance, which was being held at the Governor's mansion.

Meanwhile he and his buddy were getting ready for the big celebration dance that night. There would be plenty of girls there to give them a good sendoff. When Brainard and Frederick got there, red, white and blue streamers decorated the magnificent palace. Tables of food were laden with all kinds of food…meats, vegetables, salads, and relishes of all kinds. The dessert table was spread with delectable cakes, pies, cookies, and candies. Frederick was happy that his favorite dessert of chocolate pie piled high with whip cream was on the table.

Wondering where his father and Wee were, he scanned the crowd. All of a sudden his heart about jumped out of his chest. There standing with his family was Kat. He blinked his eyes. It couldn't be. She was a vision. She was even prettier than he remembered. There were men standing around her, vying for her attention. He said to his buddy, who was talking with another girl, "See you later."

"Frederick quickly strode over to her. The orchestra began playing The Viennese waltz. He pushed through the crowd of attentive men. He came up behind her and grabbing her small waist twirled her around facing him and swung her out on the dance floor. Holding her small waist at arms length, their eyes did the talking as they gaily waltzed around the room. The other dancers drew back watching them. An excitement filled the room at this attractive couple. Their dancing was so breathtaking. Before the song ended, Frederick danced her quickly towards the door, which led to a terrace. These moments must not be wasted by conversation. Then stopping and holding her at arms length and looking at her in the twilight, he whispered, "What a surprise!" Not saying a word she reached up cupping his face in her soft hands, pulling it down to hers. His heart began to pound. Her hair smelled of roses. She kissed him. The kiss said everything, the longing they had for each other, a kiss that said I am yours forever.

Then she laughed, saying, "Oh Frederick, you have grown a mustache since I last saw you. I like it."

"Well, I was thinking of shaving it off, but since you like it, I might keep it for awhile. It might help me keep warm in the cold North." Then looking at her, he said, "You are speaking English. How did that happen?"

"Oh there's so much to tell you Frederick. After I got to my Aunt Clare's home, she had a private tutor come everyday, so I could learn to write and speak English. My first letter I wrote to you in English, and that's how your parent's knew how to contact me."

"You mean the second letter you wrote to me. Reaching into his shirt, he pulled the lace handkerchief out with the note still wrapped in it that she had first written to him.

She covered her mouth with her hand. "Oh my knight in shining armor, how could I have forgotten about that? And to think you have carried it with you ever since."

She was so gentle and understanding. Frederick turned with a boyish grin. "You, Kat, have crept into my heart." She clasped his fingers snugly with her own, saying "And you mine, Frederick."

How could things change so completely in a few hours, he thought. He would be gone for two years. Would she wait for him? Could he bear being away from her for that long of a period of time? Oh, if he had known about her earlier. Would he still be longing for adventure and go on this expedition? Why did he always want his cake and eat it too?

Just then a spray of stars, red, white, and blue, streaked through the sky, making a whistling noise. The fireworks had started. He pulled her close to him, holding her as her body trembled a little.

His father and Wee came walking out. "We have been looking for you." They stood in awe watching the spectacular fireworks with them from the terrace overlooking the river.

Still feeling as if he was in a dream, reality crept into his brain. He dreaded tomorrow. The trip he had been so excited about was to begin, and Kat would be on her way home. Only memories would remain. When the night came to an end, and they were parting, Otto and Wee made an excuse to hail a carriage to take them to their hotel for the night.

As he and Kat sat on the railing of the terrace, he was thinking, Would she think him brash if he spoke things that were on his mind? What a pity he couldn't look into her heart and learn her hidden secrets.

"Marry me, tonight Kat," he burst out. "I have to have you for my wife before I go."

She looked at this man with a quiet passion. His presence was so electric! The man wants me now, right now for his wife. He is so gentle and sincere. "My knight in shining armor…I will accept your proposal, but I want my husband by my side, not one that will be wandering all over the world. Not a husband that might never come back!" She covered her tear filled eyes with her hands. She had never felt so exasperated in her whole life.

Frederick could not bear her being so upset. Looking at her, he said, "I will tell Lt. Greely, that I will not go then."

She looked at him. The wildness of adventure was in his eyes. To think that he cared so much for her that he was willing to sacrifice his dream. How selfish she was. If she kept him from going on this expedition, he would grow to hate her. She could never stand this. There would never be anyone for her, but Frederick. She would wait for him, wait until the end of eternity.

Looking up at him, she said, "No my dear Frederick. I want you to go. I shall be waiting when you come home. Meanwhile, I will prepare for our wedding for the love of my life…you."

Deep within him, hope took root. He impulsively took both of her hands in his. They embraced and sealed their forever love with a kiss. He lifted her up in his strong arms and carried her to a waiting carriage. Otto and Wee met them at the hotel door.

CHAPTER 79

THE VOYAGE TO THE COLD NORTH BEGINS

On July 5th, with all men on board, a small steam launch sailed into St. John's, Newfoundland. Then changing to the Proteus they dropped to anchor off Queen's wharf and awaited more supplies. The men enjoyed browsing in the various shops in Newfoundland. While shopping, Frederick purchased a beautiful but simple diamond ring for his bride to be. Inside was an inscription, saying "Forever."

On July 7th the men were ready to head their prow toward Greenland. There was a touch of sadness mingled with exultation. They were excited about speeding on to the icy north, but they were also sad at leaving loving hearts behind them in the sunny south.

Frederick was ready for this great adventure. The few scattered icebergs and remnants of the enormous ice fields were exciting to behold. He knew that two years would go quickly, and he would see his Kat again. Leaving her was something he hated to do, but the call of this expedition was something he had been waiting for all of his life. The memories of July 4th would linger in his mind forever.

DEFINITIONS OF WORDS

Angle iron	A piece of structural steel rod with an L-shaped section.
Anvil	A heavy steel faced iron block on which metal is shaped (as by hand hammering).
Bad medicine	A person who has spirits set against him.
Big Muddy River	The Missouri River. Supposedly comes from an Indian name, Pekitanoui, meaning 'muddy water'.
Black Hills	Black Hills, the home of the Sioux Indians.
blood brothers	A person bound to one by the ceremony of mingling his blood with one's own.
Breechcloth	A cloth worn about the loins to cover the buttocks.
Buffalo Man	A half human and half buffalo man. (fictional only).
Camp red with meat	A successful buffalo hunt.
Chinook	A dry, warm wind.
Cottonwoods	A poplar tree with cottony hair on its seeds (catkins.)
Coup	A plains Indian scores a coup when he touched his enemy with a coup stick (a long slender branch used in battle) lance or anything else held in the hand.
Cradleboard	A leather, pouch-like home of an Indian infant. The mother carries her child on her back. She also hung the board from a lodge-pole or from the pommel of her saddle or would prop it against a tree.

Entrails	The inner organs.
Gate of the White Buffalo	Where thousands of buffalo went.
Gulch	A ravine; a deep, steep-sided gully, with or without a stream at the bottom.
Hardtack	A large, coarse, hard unleavened bread.
Ho!	A call or cry to attract attention, as Westward ho!
Homestead Act	A homestead in the U. S. granted to a settler to be developed as a farm. Homestead Act passed in 1862 granting public land not to exceed 160 acres to any citizen or alien intending to become a citizen.
"Hownk Hownk"	Means yes, all right, I agree in Indian language.
Indian Coffee	Coffee made by a second boiling.
Indian Lore	Indian knowledge/Learning
Medicine Bag	An Indian's sac red bundle.
Oh hong	Means fish in Indian language.
Pemmican	The universal preserved food of the Indians who lived on the buffalo, and later of the mountain men and other frontiersmen who learned Indian ways. Pemmican was made from buffalo, deer or moose meat, that was jerked, pounded fine, mixed equally by weight with marrow fat and stored in parfleches or sewn into other skin sacks. Often dried berries were added, especially chokecherries and serviceberries. Preserved in this way, pemmican lasted for several years.
Plateau	An elevated tract of more or less level land.
Powwow	Social and religious events of Indians to come together to trade socialize and dance.
Purified	To free from guilt, sin, or ceremonial uncleanness.
Quiver	A case for carrying arrows.
Sagebrush	Small white or yellow flowers and a sagelike odor.
Sim-a-hi	Means grizzly.

Sioux Tribe	Indians who call themselves Dakota.
Skinny Game	An Indian game where 80 to 100 people can play. It's played with a ball and stick. You cannot touch the ball with stick. A very vigorous game.
Skirmish	A brief fight or encounter.
Smoothbore Rifle	A rifle having no grooves or ridges on the inner surface of the barrel.
Sorrel Pony	A light reddish brown horse.
Tac Ha na dahpe	Come here (in Indian language)
Thunder Stick	The Indians called their guns a Thunder Stick.
Tourniquet	A device to stop bleeding.
Travois	A travois was made by taking a pair of lodge-poles, criss-crossing the small ends on a horse's back, letting the butt ends drag behind, slinging skins or straps of skin in between and typing gear on. It was equivalent of a wagon.
Wakonda	Sun
Water Basin	Bowl to wash up in.
Werewolf	Folklore, a person changed into a wolf.

About the Author

Chastine Shumway is an author who has worn coats of many colors. She has had ink in her blood since nine years of age. She loves to write. In her golden years she is a freelance reporter, writing nonfiction and fiction articles for magazines and major newspapers throughout the United States. Research and history of the 1800's are her forte and her articles are much in demand.

She has owned several newspapers and has been editor for various newspapers in the south. The newspaper she is the proudest of was, *Teen Scenes and Family Scenes*. Elvis Presley and Mayor Loeb of Memphis wrote the send off articles for teenagers and family in the first edition.

She became well known throughout the South, for writing the best and most sought after resumes and cover letters that drew the attention of the media. She then became 'The Resume Lady' and was guest speaker at graduations, educational programs, and was a regular television guest on television. Although she no longer owns it, 'The Resume Lady' is still in business in Memphis, Tennessee. Her most treasured jewels are her family of six children. In her spare time she enjoys playing Scrabble.

She has won many awards in her writing, and has one published children's story with other authors in some Southern libraries. She gives credit to God for her talent in writing for children, young adult, and whatever stories that HE has put in her mind. She wrote *Ayoka's Prophecy* nine years ago and decided it was time to share it with others.

0-595-31460-0

Printed in the United States
20392LVS00005B/165

9 780595 314607